About the author

S M Bretherton is a writer who has been struck by her experiences of working and travelling in East and Southern Africa.

With a career spanning international development and primary education, she has written several feature articles and conducted radio interviews, a number of which have been published and broadcast in the UK and Africa.

Having recently discovered the joys of running, she is currently training for a marathon on the north-west coast of England, where she now resides with her daughter and their six-year-old Jackapoo.

HOW THE MZUNGU FINDS HER FEET

S M Bretherton

HOW THE MZUNGU FINDS HER FEET

Vanguard Press

VANGUARD PAPERBACK

© Copyright 2020
S M Bretherton

A CIP catalogue record for this title is
available from the British Library.

ISBN 978 1 784658 94 6

*Vanguard Press is an imprint of
Pegasus Elliot MacKenzie Publishers Ltd.*
www.pegasuspublishers.com

First Published in 2020

**Vanguard Press
Sheraton House Castle Park
Cambridge England**

Printed & Bound in Great Britain

Dedication

For my mum, Shirley, who may not be able to read this book but whose steadfast belief in me has played a huge part in its existence. God bless you, Mum.

Acknowledgements

I want to thank my friend, Helen Fearn, who willingly agreed to read the first chapters of this book despite being incredibly busy setting up home in France. Letting go of those first chapters into the hands of a straight-talking – the reason I chose her – critic was one of the scariest things I have done. To have her come back with a super positive response was really exciting and the main reason I continued to completion of this story. Thank you, Helen.

I also want to thank my dad – Rodney Bretherton – who has gently but regularly encouraged me to incorporate the wonderful (and not so wonderful) experiences of my time spent travelling and working in East and Southern Africa into my writing. I finally took the first step, Dad.

I want to thank my daughter, Nia, who inspires me to try to be a better human being. Never give up on your dreams and always remember you are precious.

Thanks to my friends, Marie Daniel and John Watson, who listened enthusiastically and gave their considered opinions on some of the practical aspects of my work, in particular the title and the blurb. Thank you so much. I value you both.

In addition, thank you to my good friend, Lesley, who helped with the proof reading. Your encouraging words came just at the right time.

Last but not least, thank you to Rose Kalemera, a truly inspiring, hardworking and beautiful human being who I am privileged to call my friend. May all your visions materialise.

Chapter 1

Ruth stood waiting and whilst she waited her eyes were drawn downwards towards her throbbing feet. She contemplated the ridiculous sight of white flesh bulging out between the thin red straps of her new sandals, sandals that had looked elegant and well-fitted when she boarded the plane in Glasgow nearly twenty hours earlier. She was transfixed, fascinated by feet that seemed to be growing before her eyes, wondering how, when the time came to move, she was going to put one in front of the other.

Ruth had been waiting for some time. She couldn't go anywhere because she didn't know where to go. The email she had received three days earlier, whose contents she tried visualising to make sure she hadn't missed some vital piece of information, said that she would be met by a VSO in-country staff member. She had been scanning the arrivals hall in vain, watching emotional reunions with more than a tinge of sadness. Unsurprisingly, her presence seemed to be arousing some curiosity and she was beginning to feel conspicuous. She tried to meet the bold stares with a smile which was not, on the whole, reciprocated. Her feet provided a welcome distraction.

Then it happened. Three single, ear-piercing shots in close succession sent everyone except Ruth diving, face down, to the ground.

The hall fell into total silence, broken only by the sudden echoing sound of a man's heavy footsteps running across the exposed floor, shouting as he ran and brandishing a pistol poised for action. Not a soul moved, not even to look at him. He ran towards the exit, out of the glass doors, and then he was gone. And there was nothing more.

For a few seconds it was as if no one dared breathe. Then slowly, cautiously, people began picking themselves up off the floor and helping others around them to stand up. They began talking again. Some looked quizzically over in Ruth's direction. Some even giggled. Ruth could only stand there rooted to the spot, her long, wavy, red hair and pale skin shouting out, "Look at me, look at me!" In, out. In, out, came the rhythm of her breathing as she brought her awareness back to her body, her heartbeat thudding in her ears all the while.

"Ruth Ross?"

Someone had spoken to her. It was a Scottish accent belonging to a very tall, bearded man dressed in dark blue chinos and a white T-shirt, with the purple lettering VSO emblazoned across the front.

She nodded, still trying to make some sense out of what had just happened.

"Welcome to Uganda," the man said.

Chapter 2

Doug was in no mood to hang about. He had heard that LRA rebels were operating closer to Entebbe airport in recent months and he knew how quickly things could go wrong. He had seen it happen and he was in no hurry to see it again. Ruth was so green she would only be a liability if things got out of hand. They needed to get back to Tanzania as soon as possible.

Doug knew he should have been more welcoming but it irritated him how these youngsters chose to 'find themselves' in Africa. He resented having to spend precious time and resources on travelling to Entebbe to collect them when there were people back in Mwanza who seriously needed his help. He had argued with Naomi, his boss, on several occasions about this. "Why can't these kids get themselves to Mwanza? It would be a good part of their induction," he had protested.

Naomi, of course, disagreed. She wanted her guests to experience a 'warm, African welcome'. She thought it could mean the difference between a whistle-stop tour and a longer, more meaningful stay for everyone. "Maybe this time…" she said, "… it will be a different pot of fishes." Doug smiled. Ah, Naomi and her misquoted idioms!

Ruth's question, "What the bloody hell was that all about?" had not fallen on deaf ears. He had heard it. He had simply chosen not to answer. At least not yet. He indicated for her to follow him and quickly moved towards the exit marked 'Transfers'.

It struck Ruth as extremely odd how quickly the airport appeared to settle. It was as if nothing had happened, people just going about their everyday business. All she could do was follow the back of 'beardy bloke's' head and shoulders. If she was ever going to change her mind about this leap of faith into the unknown, now was the time to do it. Beardy bloke, who had only turned around once to check on her, would probably neither know nor care. He hadn't even offered to carry her bag! But how could she think of abandoning her adventure before it had started? Surely, she was made of stronger stuff. A good sleep and a shower was all she needed and she would be back on track. Anyway, going straight back to the mess she had left behind was not an option.

Tightening her grip around the worn handle of her leather suitcase, Ruth pulled herself up tall and continued tottering after her so-called companion.

The travellers stepped out of the air-conditioned building into the hot African morning. It felt wonderful at first, like the first few minutes inside a sauna as the water quickly dries off the skin.

Very soon, though, Ruth found herself succumbing to the sun's power, like too much wine on a hot day gradually seeping into every part of the body, relaxing her limbs and causing her eyelids to droop.

"Carry your bag, madam?"

Ruth heard the words then felt a small tug on the handle of her suitcase. She turned to see a boy of about fourteen, his hair, face, arms and legs a greyish colour, his clothes shabby and his feet bare. The sight of him might have drawn a smile if his poverty was not so palpable.

The boy grinned at Ruth with his mouth, but not his eyes, she noticed. They both kept a firm hold on the handle of her case. Beyond them a group of younger boys stood watching.

Not usually stuck for words, Ruth felt vulnerable and inadequate. "It's okay, I can manage, thank you," she said, smiling weakly. But the boy was not giving up. Taking full advantage of that split second of indecision, he gripped harder, pulling the suitcase towards him whilst repeating his request, more insistently this time. Anxiously, Ruth's eyes searched ahead for her guide. Why hadn't he waited? And why hadn't he told her his name?

"If you're gonna be here for a wee while, lass, you're gonna have to toughen up!"

Beardy bloke appeared and his presence seemed to have an immediate effect on the boys. There was a swift exchange of words and the boys turned their attention elsewhere.

"Aren't they just trying to earn a living?" Ruth asked.

"Aye, maybe so, lass, but have you ever heard of the expression, 'Give him an inch and he'll take a mile'? There are other ways to help. You'll find out. Right, let's get going. We've got a plane to catch."

Ruth had to squint to see through the shimmering haze that made her surroundings move in a hypnotic dance.

15

Keeping her eyes firmly fixed on beardy bloke's large frame, she hobbled behind. "I'm tougher than you think, beardy bloke," she muttered.

The plane they were due to take from Entebbe to Mwanza across Lake Victoria was delayed, a fact that neither seemed to disturb nor surprise the waiting passengers. Inside the transfer hut, Ruth sat cross-legged on the floor. She watched fellow travellers pick up a Uganda Airlines brochure to fan themselves and she followed suit. The effect was negligible.

Beardy bloke handed Ruth a warm Pepsi Cola from the out-of-order refrigerator, and she savoured its sweet, sharp gas with every mouthful. He chose to remain standing, making him appear even taller. What an odd couple they must look, thought Ruth: she with her unkempt mass of red hair and he over six feet tall with a bushy beard. Since it was impossible to make conversation with him as they were, and Ruth was too lethargic to stand, she allowed her thoughts to drift. Smells of body odour wafted up her nostrils as her head tipped backwards and her eyes closed. She could hear chattering all around her and though no expert, she was sure she heard the sounds and intonations of several languages being spoken.

Doug stood, eyes fixed on the glinting lump of metal that taunted him from the other side of the glass pane. He was hot and tired. He never got used to the waiting around that seemed to be an inevitable part of this thankless journey. All he wanted was a cold Stella and the company of his sweet Khadeja – Khadeja, who had certainly made his life more bearable these past few months. Doug thought he had died and gone to heaven every time he was with Khadeja who mesmerised him with her strong, beautifully curved body and sensuous lips. He could see her now, standing there smiling at him, waiting for him. "Come to Khadeja, Dougee," she would say.

Doug sighed and scratched his head. He looked down at his ward, wondering how long this one would last. Judging by her absurd footwear, not very long.

Chapter 3

Ruth hoped to engage beardy bloke in conversation on the short flight to Mwanza but, after seeing her seated, he moved on down the aisle towards the back of the plane, leaving her perplexed. She was convinced her red sandals were to blame. Still, even taking them into consideration, she felt she deserved to be treated with a little more courtesy. After all, she did not have to make the decision to uproot and leave all her home comforts to come out to Africa. Surely beardy bloke could have shown a little appreciation of that. Ruth sighed and stared out of the plane's tiny window onto the great expanse of blue below. Lake Victoria grew smaller and smaller as they ascended until it disappeared under a blanket of billowing white clouds whose brightness dazzled her.

The next thing she knew, Ruth was being nudged gently by a stewardess. The plane had landed and her fellow passengers were making their way to the exits. Groggily, Ruth waited until it was beardy bloke's turn to pass along the gangway. Although he acknowledged her with a curt nod, he did not attempt to make conversation but simply moved along the plane with the clear expectation that she would follow on.

Ruth was irritated but when she and Doug emerged out of Mwanza airport, her attention shifted immediately.

She had finally arrived at her destination. And what a destination! She was confronted by a riot of colour: from the intricately patterned clothes worn by people in every direction she looked and the exotic fruits and vegetables lined up along the kerbs, as well as on rickety wooden roadside stalls, to the rich terracotta hue of the soil they walked on. And all of this against a backdrop of loud pulsating rhythms of African dance music blaring out from the dala dalas – the mini-bus 'taxis' – littering the roadway as well as the melange of rich smells, the like of which Ruth had never experienced. This was indeed Africa as she had imagined her! This was the Africa she had seen played out on her television screen in her cramped, red-brick, mid-terrace and she wanted to inhale it all in and absorb its soul, allowing it to pervade her very being...

"Look, lassie, no disrespect but I hope you're not gonna drop like the last one," beardy bloke called back to her over his shoulder.

Reluctantly adjusting her focus, Ruth was confused. "Sorry?" she queried. What could he mean?

"The smell," he clarified, wafting his hand in a circular motion around him. "You wouldn't be the first to baulk on arrival. Believe it or not, you get to like it after a while."

Not wanting to think what her own aroma was like at that particular moment, a wry smile passed across Ruth's lips. "Oh, I can believe it all right," she responded.

Beardy bloke marched on and an awestruck Ruth followed. Past the queues and the muddle of hangers-on they went, Ruth feeling somehow bound together with the people who happened, fleetingly, to occupy the same space as her. She wanted to seem adventurous in their eyes. She had left Scotland to come to Africa – this other world that had been turning without her and would continue to turn when she had gone. Her adventure truly had begun.

Chapter 4

Naomi sat bent over her wobbly desk where she had been since seven a.m. Deep in concentration, she was still clutching the chai that Bwana Rutiga had boiled for her on her arrival, occasionally sipping the tepid liquid from the non-chipped side of the mug. She was reading through a final draft of the latest donor report she and her skeleton staff had spent weeks preparing for the Danish Development Agency (DANIDA). It was almost finished, just a few tweaks here and there, then she would be able to get back to the real work.

As Naomi shifted position, the table wobbled yet again. Sighing, she reached for the folded paper under the leg closest to her. Curiously she unfolded it. The paper bore the name of a cousin who was living overseas but had returned and was now a big shot hotel manager in Dar es Salaam. She remembered her mother scribbling down his details and pushing it into her hand before she left their home village, "just in case". Naomi sighed, refolded the paper and pushed it back into position, applying pressure to the table and at the same time knocking over the bucket she had placed strategically to catch drips of water from the leaking roof. The rainy season had just started and so far there was no prospect of getting the roof fixed. If only she could include fixtures and fittings in their funding requests. Maybe, she mused, if the people in these far-off lands were to experience for themselves, the infrastructural challenges she and so many like her faced on a daily basis, they might reconsider their reluctance to fund capital expenditure. It was so difficult to run effective programmes when you were struggling with leaks, broken furniture and an intermittent electricity supply.

Pulling herself up straight, Naomi refocused her attention on her reading and resolved to stay positive. After all, these problems were nothing new.

At eight-fifteen, Freja Johansson walked in, sheepishly glancing over to Naomi's desk.

Looking up, Naomi greeted her, "Habari za asubuhi?"

"Good morning." Freja returned the greeting, whilst uttering some half-hearted excuse for her tardiness. Naomi had heard it all before. She had been offered Freja's services by the DANIDA representative in Tanzania – who also happened to be Freja's father – as part of the donor support package and was still trying to make up her mind about the usefulness of this so-called support. Naomi could not stop herself wondering what would make a young person – a guest in her country – feel they could adopt such a careless approach to the lives of her fellow Tanzanians. It was Naomi's opinion that if Freja spent more time with the locals instead of socialising with expatriates down at the Lakeside hotel bar, she might begin to understand the people she was supposedly here to help.

Naomi had heard that Freja was spending a good deal of time hanging around the Ramada hotel lately where Andwele, Naomi's youngest son, was a trainee manager.

Naomi loved her son but she knew that he had let his relative success go to his head as far as the young ladies were concerned. Why couldn't he have followed in his brother's footsteps? Julius had just qualified as a criminal lawyer, a position that commanded a good deal of respect, not to mention the salary. Andi, on the other hand, seemed to attract attention wherever he went and mostly the wrong kind of attention in Naomi's opinion. She hoped and prayed he was being careful. She did not want him to break anyone's heart but neither did she want him being trapped before he was ready.

Oh yes, she knew what the local girls wanted, or thought they wanted. If only they could have access to the same levels of education as the boys, they would not have to rely on dirty tictacs – another Naomi-ism – to get their man and secure a future for themselves.

"What do you want me to do Mama Julius?" Freya asked.

Wishing Freja could show a little more enthusiasm, Naomi handed over the document she was working on. "If you could just carry on from this page checking for any typing errors or things that don't make sense. Then that's it, I think; we're ready to send it off. Amen."

As Freja took the wad of paper from Naomi, they both heard the sound of Gilbert's four-by-four pulling up outside the gate.

***

Ruth was not surprised when beardy bloke disappeared almost immediately on their arrival in Mwanza, after dutifully handing her over to the VSO driver, a smiling, stocky, shiny-skinned man named Gilbert who insisted on calling her "Miss Ruth". She was sorry she had not made a good first impression on beardy bloke but decided not to dwell on it. As they pulled into the small courtyard, she set eyes on two of the most stunning women she had ever seen. Both were tall. One was African and clearly more mature in years with smooth, glowing skin, bold features and elaborately braided hair. The other, a much slimmer build and younger with tanned skin and hair the colour of white chocolate that was fashionably cut into a mid-length bob.

The African woman was classically dressed in western style with court shoes, a knee-length skirt and a loose blouse. The blonde woman wore a mini skirt and vest top with sports flip-flops. The African woman was smiling warmly whilst the other woman's eyes were hidden behind her round sunglasses and her mouth was set straight. Feeling travel weary and a little intimidated, Ruth climbed down from the rickety jeep – almost knocking the broken wing mirror completely off its hinge in the process – and walked towards the women, her hand outstretched.

Naomi was first to step forward. "Karibu sana. You're very welcome," she said as she took Ruth's hand in hers. Naomi was adept at using both languages when dealing with Mzungus.

"Thank you. I'm very happy to be here," Ruth replied and she really meant it.

Comforted by Naomi's warmth, Ruth turned to greet the other woman who, she found, had turned her back and was making her way inside.

The vegetable samosas and bottles of soda on offer inside the office were welcome refreshment. Ruth had eaten very little since leaving home, preferring to settle her nerves on the flight with vodka tonics. A combination of fatigue, alcohol and hunger was beginning to take its toll and she was struggling to converse. Noticing her difficulties, Naomi suggested they talk again later when Ruth had rested a while.

"Freja, go with Gilbert and show Ruth to her hotel, please."

"Of course Mama Julius," Freja replied, with raised eyes. Her expression did not escape Ruth.

***

Freja was in a bad mood. This new arrival from Britain had better know her place. After four months, Freja was used to being the Mzungu around the place. She liked the attention her blonde locks and icy blue eyes attracted. But there was something about Ruth that unsettled her. Like Freja, Ruth was tall and slim, her fair skin, not yet kissed by the African sun, was attractively dotted with reddish brown freckles and her long red hair was tinged with golden highlights that flickered as the light caught them. The thing that peeved Freja the most, however, was that Ruth was clearly not aware of her good looks and that, Freja knew, would make her more attractive to men.

Freja would have to up her game now there was competition. The attention she got from men proved a welcome distraction that kept her going whilst she was stuck in this 'dive of a place' following a deal she made with her father. She wasn't about to let Ruth spoil her fun.

"Where are you from?" Ruth's question interrupted Freja's thoughts.

"Denmark."

"Oh nice. I've never been there myself. How come you came to Tanzania?"

"My dad…"

Ruth looked for more.

"He runs the Danish aid agency here. He thought it would be a good experience for me." Freja's reply came back monotone.

"And is it?"

"I suppose. It depends on your point of view." Freja was feeling irritated by all the questions. Why did Ruth have to be so nosey?

Sensing the hostility in Freja's voice, Ruth decided not to ask any more questions. This girl was not going to be easy to get to know.

Instead, Ruth focused her attention on Mwanza town, observing with great interest the mish-mash of Islamic and colonial-style architecture passing them by; every now and again punctuated by a soulless, modern building. Potholes in the road sent them jumping up and down in their seats and other vehicles cut them up, honking their horns loudly as they did so. When Gilbert stopped at traffic lights, his vehicle was quickly surrounded by pedlars of all ages selling everything from monkey nuts to chamois leathers. The pedlars had spotted Ruth from a distance and flocked excitedly to the open windows, each trying to thrust their wares up to her face in front of the others. Freja kept her head facing forward without so much as a glance in their direction.

"These look really good but I don't have any need for them at the moment," Ruth said politely.

Freja felt sick. Is this woman for real? Just then she caught sight of Andi and all thoughts of Ruth disappeared.

Standing on the steps of the Ramada Hotel, talking to the gardener, Andi was looking as handsome as ever. Having to keep on the good side of Naomi was a small price to pay for being able to associate with her son. Just look at him! Freja rested her eyes on Andi's athletic physique, braided ponytail and fake Ray bans. The crisp white shirt with turned-up cuffs and black waistcoat made him look even sharper. Freja could hardly wait for Gilbert to pull up outside the hotel before throwing her door open, jumping down and rushing over to Andi without so much as a second thought for Ruth. Andi seemed pleased to see her too, planting a kiss on both cheeks as she lifted her face up to his.

Ruth struggled to pick up her suitcase and various bits of hand luggage. Gilbert rushed to do it for her, but she was insisting he could leave her with the bags and go back to see if Naomi needed him. The two of them stood, like this, on the roadside, each trying to make the other understand, the noise from passing traffic not making things any easier.

Suddenly there was a scream and the sound of screeching brakes. Which came first, Ruth wasn't sure. Within seconds, the monstrous chicken truck responsible was surrounded by men, women and children pushing to see what had happened.

"Kusaidia!" Someone ran over to them shouting for help.

Ruth hesitated. She really had intended to leave the job behind but someone was in trouble and what if she was the only one on the spot who could help? Letting go of her suitcase, she ran over to the truck. She had to force her way through the gathering crowd, all the while her pulse racing and her stomach flipping. Reaching the back wheel of the truck, Ruth bent down to see what she could.

Nothing could have prepared Ruth for the sight before her. A woman's head and torso lay just behind the truck's nearside wheel, blood pouring out from where her lower limbs should have been. Ruth gagged as she caught sight of the missing limbs across the undercarriage. Two men, one on either side, looked at her, shaking their heads. There was nothing to be done.

Wailing began to fill the air, reaching a crescendo, as news rippled back through the gathered crowd. Slowly straightening up, Ruth came face-to-face with a teenage girl whose hands were clasped over her mouth and whose eyes were filled with panic. Ruth took hold of her and the girl began to shake uncontrollably.

"I'm so sorry," Ruth whispered.

Collapsing into Ruth, the girl released a sound, the like of which Ruth had never heard. Two women came forward and led her away.

Gradually the crowd began to disperse. The bloody body parts were dragged onto the grass verge at the far side of the road. Someone had called for an ambulance but it could be some time before it arrived, Ruth was told.

"They will collect the body later, Miss Ruth," Gilbert informed her. "This is not a good welcome to Mwanza. Please forgive."

Ruth was spent. She gave in to Gilbert's insisting and allowed him to carry all her luggage into the hotel.

Climbing the steps up to the foyer, Ruth sensed she was being watched. She looked up into the brown eyes of a stranger, who smiled and winked at her, but she was too weary to care.

Freja – who was still standing by – cared very much.

Chapter 5

After politely declining Freja's somewhat insincere suggestion to dine together, Ruth, at last, found herself alone. Freja had gone off happily, seemingly unmoved by the events of the afternoon. Ruth, on the other hand, could think of nothing else. At least in her room, she could be herself.

Ruth's sandal straps were firmly embedded in the flesh of her swollen feet and she had to prise them off, leaving deep imprints as she did so – a mocking reminder of her frivolous, totally unsuitable choice. Perhaps her presence in Africa was equally misplaced. Gingerly, she placed her feet down heel to toe, savouring the soothing feeling of the cold, hard floor on her bare skin.

The phone rang, making Ruth jump. Keeping her feet firmly planted, she leaned back across the bed, reaching for the handset.

"Hello, lass."

Beardy bloke! What did he want?

"It's Doug," he continued "Just wanted to check you've settled in okay?"

"Yes, thanks, Doug."

"I'm in reception just now. Do you fancy a wee drink and a chat?"

Well, it certainly sounded like his voice but had Doug had a personality transplant? It was on the tip of Ruth's tongue to decline his offer but something told her not to.

"Okay, you go ahead and get one in and I'll join you in five," she said.

Before making her way down, Ruth dug out a pair of flip flops from near the top of her case and reverently slipped them onto her grateful feet.

Surprisingly, Doug turned out to be really good company. At least they understood each other's sense of humour, and he was much more relaxed than he had been earlier in the day.

"I heard what happened," Doug said. "Quite an induction!"

Ruth paused for a while. "She was someone's wife, mum, sister maybe," she said thoughtfully. "It must be up there with one of the worst things I've ever seen and that's saying something." She went on. "I really don't know if I'm cut out for this."

"Oh?" Doug looked up, waiting for an explanation.

"Well, for starters, look at my choice of footwear and then there's how I reacted – or rather didn't react – in the airport when the gun went off, and to top it all, I seem to have made an instant enemy out of Freja without even trying," Ruth lamented.

Doug snorted. "Don't give that one a second thought. Believe me, she won't you."

"Why do you say that?"

"That lassie is irrelevant. It's Naomi who keeps that place going and Naomi alone. You'd be a fool to change your plans because of the other one."

Bit harsh, thought Ruth but kept her opinion to herself. Still, maybe there was something in it. Perhaps Freja was just not important in Ruth's plans and, if they could learn to co-exist without stepping on each other's toes, maybe it could work.

"I'll give myself a couple of weeks," Ruth said, "then I'll decide."

"Good idea, lass."

Ruth and Doug sat in silence with their thoughts. He had a habit of pushing his hair back off his forehead and when he did so, just for a second, Ruth thought she saw something familiar in the high forehead and green eyes. Just as quickly, she dismissed the thought. With her stomach full of samaki and rice, Ruth felt satisfied and ready for a drink. She took a cigarette from Doug when offered and he noticed her hand shaking as she plucked it from the packet he held out. It wasn't the only thing he noticed… A tall figure at the far end of the bar had been watching their whole encounter with great interest.

***

When Freja arrived at the Ramada, unannounced, smelling fresh with a full face of makeup and wearing her lilac halter-neck mini dress with matching high heels, she spotted Andi leaning on the bar totally absorbed in something at the other end of the room. Following his line of sight, she soon realised what, or rather who, was holding his attention. That Ruth woman was going to have to watch herself, that was for sure. If she thought she had any chance with Andi, she had another think coming.

"Andi!" Freja called as she walked over to him, giving him a hug and planting herself firmly between him and the view he had been so much admiring.

Andi had no choice but to look at Freja. She was gorgeous! As she spoke, he became transfixed by her pale pink lip gloss, watching her lips move but not heeding her words. He looked into her blue eyes and thought he must be a fool. His friends could not believe he had not snapped her up already. But Andi liked a challenge. What fun was it if a woman threw herself at you, even if she did look like Freja Johansson? He smiled, and she carried on talking.

"Okay, Andi, I'm off. See you at the club later?" Freja's eyes widened as she stared at him expectantly.

"Maybe. I'm working late though," he replied.

Freja laughed dismissively, waved her hand and called out, "See you there." She was one hundred per cent confident he would show up. How could he not?

Andi, however, had no intention of going to meet Freja. He was cross that he had allowed himself to be distracted and now the other two had gone, and he didn't even know if they had left together or not. Irritated, he turned back towards the restaurant kitchen and the remainder of his shift.

Chapter 6

It was gone midnight when a weary Andi finally arrived home. If he had not been given a lift, it would have been even later. Still, with any luck he would soon have wheels of his own.

"Andi, is that you?" Julius' voice called from the kitchen. His brother often worked late too. "Come and sit and eat with me. Gloria has left something for us."

Andi removed his shoes, swapping them for a pair of moccasins that he was accustomed to wearing inside, and entered the compact kitchen where Julius was busy eating a plate of ugali and bean stew.

"No nyama choma today, my brother," Julius remarked, "but it's still good."

Andi washed his hands, took a glass from the drainer and filled it with the remainder of the beer from the can his brother had started. Setting the glass down on the kitchen table opposite Julius, he returned to the cooker to plate himself up the leftover food.

"So, my brother. What sort of a day did you have?" Julius asked.

"Sawa sawa," Andi replied, clearly underwhelmed, "I think I am getting to grips with the job." There was sarcasm in his tone.

"It's a good job, Andi, you could do a lot worse."

"Yeah, and I could do a lot better too." Andi savoured the beer and began to tuck in.

"You know, if you can just keep your head down, work hard and get the grades, this could lead to bigger and better things," Julius went on. "Who knows, you might end up manager of The Kilimanjaro Hotel in Dar!" he coaxed, giving his little brother's baseball cap a tug.

"Hey!" Andi dodged. "Never mind the Kili, I'm aiming for London or New York! Can you imagine?"

"You're not still hankering after that dream, are you?"

"Of course! Why not?"

"You know mother will cry."

"She will. But imagine what she will say when she comes to stay and gets the best penthouse suite there is!" Andi grinned.

"You dream, brother. You dream. Me, I prefer to concentrate on what I have here."

"That's why you will still be slogging away at a desk in downtown Mwanza whilst I am making a name for myself around the world."

Julius laughed. "Whatever you say, Andi. Whatever you say."

The brothers teased each other good-naturedly until Julius grew too tired to stay and bid his brother goodnight.

Andi knew that Julius would never take him seriously but he meant to do what he said. Andwele – the name Naomi had given him – meant 'brought by God' and he wore it with total confidence in its justification. He had it all planned out and he would do whatever it took to make his dream happen. Sure, Freja was hot but he had seen the way that this new British girl had looked at him today in the hotel lobby, and he had a feeling that his dream might just be one step closer to becoming a reality.

Andi's cell phone buzzed next to him. Glancing down, he saw the name flashing up on the screen and picked up.

"How are things going?" the familiar female voice at the other end of the line asked.

"Patience, patience," he replied. "We'll get there, don't worry."

"Are you still sure you want to do this?"

"Of course. Stop worrying. Give Kemi a kiss for me. Tell her Daddy misses her. I will see you soon."

"Okay. Goodnight."

"Goodnight, mpenzi. Lala salama."

Chapter 7

Ruth woke up to bright sunlight pouring through her window and filling the room. She could hear voices outside and the sound of traffic. It was Saturday and the only appointment she had was lunch with Naomi at the hotel. Eyes still half shut, Ruth rolled over to pick up her watch from the bedside cabinet. It was five a.m. Too early for breakfast.

Ten minutes later, the entire contents of her suitcase spilled out over her bed, Ruth was pulling on her running shorts and vest. What better way to shake off the stiffness from the long journey and see a bit of Mwanza at the same time? Her feet were still sore from their ordeal with the red, strappy sandals but the swelling had gone down. She massaged Vaseline into them – a tip she had picked up from her dad – before gently pulling on her sports socks and trainers. She had no idea where she was going but Ruth was not going to let that stop her. She pulled her hair up into a ponytail, grabbed her room keys and made her way down to the lobby.

Downstairs was quiet. Ruth was browsing the rack of brochures by the reception desk, looking for a street map of Mwanza, when she heard a voice behind her.

"Good morning, madam."

She turned around and found herself face-to-face with the guy who had winked at her on the steps the day before. This time he was dressed in shorts and a T-shirt and wearing a baseball cap with the letters 'NYC' across the top.

"Good morning," Ruth answered.

"I'm Andi, manager-in-training here. I hope you are finding everything to your satisfaction."

Ruth was staring. It was hard not to stare. Pulling herself together, she smiled and said, "Hi, I'm Ruth and yes thank you. Everything is great." She could mention the greenish water coming from her tap later.

"It looks like we're both going for a jog. Shall we go together?" It was a question but Andi said it as though he already knew the answer.

Ruth hesitated. She had meant to be independent. But then, what harm could it do, and she definitely needed someone to show her around a bit. She nodded. "Okay, that would be great."

Andi insisted they drive out of the town a bit. He said that the roads were uneven and you could not see much anyway. He drove one of the hotel minibuses. "We use them for airport pickups," he explained as they climbed in. Unlike the vehicle Gilbert drove, this minibus was new with smart leather seats, air conditioning and fitted with radio and CD player that Andi switched on as soon as he got in. He had brought towels from the hotel and spread them over the seats which were already burning from the morning heat. It was humid and Ruth was sweating. The air conditioning was very welcome. Even a new vehicle, though, could not avoid the potholes that seemed to litter every road. As they drove through the town, sounds of the popular dance rhythms accompanied their journey.

Spotting children everywhere, some sitting, some still sleeping but all of them dressed in tattered, dirty clothing, Ruth asked, "Why are there so many of them?"

"These are street children," Andi explained. "Orphans. Their parents are dead – most of them from AIDS."

"Is there any help?"

"Yes, there are some small organisations trying to help. They get local women to cook a meal for them and some have a house where they can shelter a few, but there are too many for them to help everyone."

Ruth was curious. "What about school?"

"These kids are not in school."

"What happens to them?"

"Some of them steal for older boys and men and they get a few pennies for that. Some of them go to the beer halls where they mix with men who abuse them or make them watch pornographic films and drink. In the end most of them get sick and die."

"That's awful!" Ruth gasped.

"That's how it is here," Andi said in a flat tone. "There are a few lucky ones who are taken into small projects by some church groups or projects funded from abroad like my mom's and they do escape."

"Where does your mum work?"

Andi laughed. "VSO. She's your boss."

Andi parked up at the foot of a small hill just outside the town centre. It was a demanding run, and Ruth could not talk much. She was going to need time to acclimatise to the weather and the altitude in East Africa. When they reached the summit, the pair paused for a while to look out over the lake and the town below them. Ruth had heard Mwanza referred to as the 'Rock City' and from her vantage point, she could see why. In every direction, she could see rocks of all shapes and sizes.

Halfway down the hill, Andi suggested they stop and stretch. Ruth found herself enjoying the tingling sensation she got each time Andi's hand made contact with her arm or leg or back. What was she thinking? She had only been here a day! Falling for her boss's son was not a good idea whichever way you looked at it.

Back at the hotel, the two parted company, with promises to meet up again later on.

"Great workout," Andi called after Ruth as she sprang up the staircase, almost tripping when she turned to quickly glance in his direction, just catching him wink at her again.

***

"You've met my youngest son then?" Naomi asked when they were seated on the terrace under a sunshade at midday.

Ruth looked up. She wanted to gauge Naomi's feelings so she would know how to answer her.

"Yes. He was very kind and showed me around Mwanza a bit this morning," Ruth replied.

Naomi was smiling. Ruth's blush had not gone unnoticed. "He's a good boy," she said. "You will meet the older one this evening and my husband if you are free and would like to come home and eat with us?"

Amused by the thought that she might not be free, Ruth accepted the invitation. "I would love to come," she said. "Thank you so much for inviting me."

"Karibu sana. Now, tell me a bit about yourself, Ruth," Naomi continued.

Ruth panicked. "What would you like to know?" she asked, stalling for time.

"Well, about your family first."

Okay, that's not too difficult, thought Ruth. I don't have to go into too many details. "Well, there's Mum and Dad and…' She wanted to say 'my sister' but decided against it. '…they live in Scotland."

"I never got chance to go to Scotland," Naomi said. "I studied at Cardiff University in Wales. It was a long way from Scotland." She laughed. "What about your work? Did you have a job in Scotland?"

"Oh yes. I have been working as a nurse in the A&E department in a hospital," Ruth went on.

"You didn't like it?" Naomi seemed disturbed.

"Well, 'like' is not the word but yes, it's a good job. It's very stressful at times though, and I had a particularly difficult year personally, so I decided it would be better for the job and for me if I took some time out."

41

"I see." Naomi was thoughtful. "Why us? Why Tanzania?"

Naomi's questions would normally have felt intrusive and threatening but she had such a way about her, such a warm manner and her eyes showed genuine interest in what Ruth had to say.

"I'm not sure really. The most obvious place to go would have been Kenya but I didn't want to do the obvious. One of my colleagues is from Tanzania and she used to talk about the country like she was so proud to come from here. She had a really gentle manner and a thoughtfulness I really admired, and I thought if Tanzanians are like that, I think I will be happy there." Ruth half laughed at her own words.

But Naomi was listening intently and clearly impressed. "Of course, we are not all the same but we Tanzanians *are* proud of our country. Everyone I know who went to study abroad came back again. It's a good thing. We need all their skills to help with the problems we are facing here."

Ruth nodded thoughtfully.

"But we need to get you some Swahili lessons," Naomi said.

"Definitely," Ruth agreed. "I would love to learn."

"And I know just the person," Naomi continued, thinking how refreshing it was to see some enthusiasm from her visitor. Maybe Ruth's arrival might be a blessing for VSO and her family all in one, she thought.

After Naomi had gone, Ruth stayed out on the terrace soaking up the peace and the sunshine and reading a book, though she couldn't remember a word of what she read. Her mind wandered back to the strained look on her father's face when they had said goodbye at the airport.

Ruth's dad had been her hero for most of her life. For as long as she could remember, they had crept out of the house together in the early mornings at weekends to go swimming, cycling or for long walks with their dog, Mutt. Dad was renowned for his short cuts that were never short and they had been lost for hours on several occasions. She smiled as she remembered the time they were halfway across a field when they discovered it was home to a territorial bull who had spotted them and was about to charge. Dad had whisked her up over his shoulder, running back to the gate, almost throwing her over as they reached it and just managing to get himself over before the angry bull arrived, snorting heavily.

Ruth smiled as she remembered how her dad had a habit of singing around the house. His songs were mostly amusing, with the exception of one. Ruth could neither understand why he sang it nor why he found it funny. She had to hide her tears when he sang the words:

'Oh my darling,
Oh my darling,
Oh my darling, Clementine.
Thou art lost and gone forever,
Dreadful sorry Clementine.'

In her childish mind she swapped 'darling' for 'daughter'.

Then he would continue to cheerfully deliver the final lines of the well-known ditty:

'So I kissed her little sister,
Soon forgot my Clementine,'

leaving Ruth in torment every time.

Of course, Dad never knew she felt like that. To him it was just a bit of fun. She doubted whether she could have explained her feelings to him anyway since the topic of her late sister was taboo in their house.

Reflecting on how one single, tragic event can affect so many people's lives irreversibly, Ruth wondered about the young girl she had held the day before and what the dead woman meant to her. What scars would her untimely death leave on this girl and others who knew and loved her? Once the rawness had gone, they would all have to get on with day-to-day living as Ruth's family had done. Then, what had happened would no longer be dominant and they would have to each find their own way of living with it, or not. It was as simple as that. Yesterday's news. Nothing more to be done.

Chapter 8

When Gilbert arrived at six p.m., Ruth was in her room. She had gone up to shower and get ready at five-thirty p.m. in bright daylight and at six the darkness seemed to come out of nowhere, turning everything from day to night as if someone had pulled a black curtain across the sky.

Gilbert and Ruth travelled companionably through the badly lit town centre, heading south out along the lake shore. There were still plenty of children out, wandering about, some sitting or lying on flattened cardboard boxes and bits of newspapers, others standing on corners, huddled together, heads bent inwards, clearly focused on something of interest. Andi had told Ruth they would be sniffing glue or gasoline.

After some twenty minutes, Gilbert pulled off the main road onto a side track that led slightly uphill to a small development of white-washed bungalows.

"Mama Julius lives here," he announced. "She is expecting you."

Thanking him, Ruth got out of the vehicle and made her way up the attractive paving that was half illuminated by Gilbert's one working headlight. As Ruth approached the front of the property, Naomi opened the door and called out in welcome.

"Karibu sana."

Inside, the family were gathered, all standing up waiting for Ruth as if she were a VIP. She was introduced to them one by one and then offered a seat that had clearly been left especially for her. It was only after she sat down that the others followed suit. The sight of Freja at one end of the room unnerved Ruth a little.

Naomi's husband, Salvatore, was charming and very attentive, as were Julius and Andi. Freja, less so. Indeed, after not too long, she complained of feeling unwell and asked Andi to drive her home.

In Andi's absence, Ruth, Salvatore and Julius talked about the British weather, football and the queen whilst Naomi, Gloria and the house girl, Sylvia, continued preparing food in the kitchen. Salvatore spoke English with ease and he showed himself to be knowledgeable about all kinds of subjects. Clearly very proud of his home, his wife and sons, he showed Ruth around, stopping at every family photograph and artefact to relate their back-story to his attentive guest. Julius was a little more reserved but pleasant nevertheless.

"We did all of this ourselves," Salvatore announced as he spread his arms out wide to encompass the contents of his home.

"It really is beautiful," Ruth responded, bringing a huge smile of satisfaction to Bwana Rwechungura's handsome face. Ruth could see why Naomi had been drawn to him. It was Ruth's opinion that together they made an elegant and formidable couple who would certainly turn heads.

The last part of the bungalow to be shown off was the wide hallway that led from the sitting room to the intricately carved wooden front door. Hanging on the white wall next to the door was a large wooden cross. Reaching out to trace its smooth contours, Ruth admired the rich colour and quality finish. Neatly resting under one of the outstretched arms was a plaque that read:

"Help us use our lives to give a voice to the voiceless and to bring hope to the destitute."

"Welcome to the table!" Naomi's voice called from the lounge. The three turned away from the cross and its impactful message to follow the matriarch's instructions.

A huge wooden dining table was laid ready with all kinds of dishes, and Ruth was first to take her seat. Naomi sat at one end of the table and Salvatore at the other. Julius and Gloria sat together opposite Ruth and Andi's seat waited empty next to her. Another empty chair was tucked in on the bend of the oval table – Naomi had invited Doug, she explained.

"We cannot wait any longer," Naomi said. "Let's say grace."

Ruth could not remember the last time she had said grace before a meal, in primary school possibly, but there was something reassuring and inclusive in the reverence of those few moments with this family.

Roasted goat meat, chicken, rice, green banana, chapattis, a bean stew, chestnut sauce, plantain, shredded cabbage and piri piri sauce were offered around as the family chatted animatedly, flipping with ease from Swahili to English with smatterings of another language Ruth did

47

not recognise. Julius explained that it was Kihaya, the family's mother tongue. Ruth found it all fascinating and did not feel at all left out since everything was explained to her by Julius who appointed himself chief translator for the evening.

Doug turned up when the meal was well underway and was made to feel very welcome. When he greeted her, Ruth felt that flicker of recognition again but she still could not put a name to it.

Andi never returned. Ruth sensed this was a source of embarrassment to his parents. She too was disappointed. She had been looking forward to finding out more about him. What was Freja up to?

After eating, they sat in the lounge drinking Stella beer from cans. Salvatore and Doug held court with their amusing stories and exchanges about anything and everything. Ruth noticed how everyone laughed. It was proper laughter, the kind where you have to hold your belly and try to breathe. She tried to remember the last time she had laughed like that.

Eventually it was time to say goodnight, and Doug offered Ruth a lift back to the hotel. Naomi, Salvatore, Julius and Gloria walked Ruth and Doug out to his pickup. It was a warm night and the frogs chirped loudly all around them as the guests said their goodbyes.

"I will come for you at eight in the morning for church," Naomi called, leaving no room for negotiation.

Slightly taken aback – she was not used to being told what to do – Ruth hesitated then smiled and nodded.

"So, how's it going?" Doug enquired once on the road.

"You know, I think I'm gonna be okay, after all," Ruth replied.

The pair talked about home. It turned out they had a lot in common, not least their passion for Queen of the South. Football games, they were another treasured memory of times shared with her dad. Doug had left home at eighteen but somehow still managed to follow his club. He avoided answering questions about his life prior to leaving Dumfries, skilfully batting them back to Ruth who found herself revealing more than she might have wished to. Before she knew it, Doug was pulling up at the foot of the Ramada front steps.

"See you anon," he said as Ruth stepped out and leaned through the open passenger window to thank him. Doug turned to face her, and in that instant she knew exactly why he looked so familiar.

Chapter 9

"Hey! Watch out!"

Blinded by tears, Ruth almost knocked Andi over as she ran into the hotel lobby.

"Ruth? What is it? What's wrong?"

Unable to speak clearly through her sobs, Ruth allowed herself to be guided to a chair in the empty bar where she sat, head bent, tears flowing freely down her cheeks, her sobs catching in her throat.

Andi waited, confused. Doug had driven off, smiling, and yet here was Ruth, inconsolable. He sat patiently until her tears began to subside. Already angry that Freja had managed to hijack his evening, he thought this may be his second chance with Ruth.

Slowly Ruth composed herself.

"What happened to you?" she asked.

"Oh, that's another story. I'll tell you sometime," Andi replied. "But now I want to know what happened with you. Did he do something to you?"

"Oh no!" Ruth protested. "Nothing like that."

"So?" Andi's eyes were full of concern.

"He just reminded me of someone from my past," Ruth murmured.

"Just reminded?"

"Yes, it couldn't be the same person."

Ruth knew, without a doubt, that Doug was that person but she needed to get her head around that realisation before speaking to anyone about it.

It was very late but Andi was not about to let this opportunity go to waste. Gently, he ordered Ruth to stay seated whilst he went behind the bar and made them both a "very special cocktail". Taking their drinks out onto the terrace, Andi and Ruth kept each other company. When Ruth began to shiver slightly, Andi took off his jacket and placed it over her shoulders. Then, when the time felt right, he moved his chair closer to hers and put his arm around her shoulders, a gesture that met no resistance.

"You are very beautiful, Ruth," Andi said, whilst still looking out into the night sky.

Ruth laughed. "Thank you for saying it," she responded, unconvinced.

"Why do you laugh?" Andi was offended that Ruth did not take him at his word. He looked straight at her, and she could not avoid his eyes.

"No reason," she said. "It's just a very, very long time since anyone accused me of that."

"Well, it is true. I said so."

Seeing that Andi did not like to be disagreed with, Ruth smiled reassuringly then she leaned her head on his shoulder, and they sat silently watching the darkness.

After some time, Andi spoke. "Do you want to marry me?"

Ruth jolted upright. Had she heard right?

Andi looked straight at her and repeated his question. "Do you want to marry me?"

Shocked, Ruth did not know how to respond. "Have you been taking something?" she asked warily.

"Taking something? What does it mean?"

"You know, drugs…"

"No! What are you talking about? I am serious but never mind, the time is not right. We will talk about it another time. It's okay."

Andi continued to behave exactly as he had before that question came out of his mouth, his confidence undented by Ruth's reaction. It was as if the question had never been asked.

Ruth, however, suddenly felt less comfortable and soon made excuses to go up to her room.

***

On Sunday morning, not wanting to keep Naomi and Salvatore waiting, Ruth was sitting ready in the hotel reception area by seven-forty-five a.m. By eight-thirty she was beginning to feel a little conspicuous.

"Can I help, madam?" one of the receptionists asked Ruth from her position behind the desk, where she had been when Ruth first came downstairs.

"Oh, I'm waiting to be picked up. They told me eight, and I didn't want to keep them waiting," Ruth explained.

"This is Africa, madam. You will get used to it," the receptionist grinned.

Ruth felt a little foolish. She was certainly exposing herself as someone who did not know how things worked, but then again, how could she? She only arrived a few days ago.

In all her years growing up in Scotland, Ruth had never experienced so many cars and people trying to get to church. Salvatore was directed onto a vast, bumpy area of wasteland by a teenage boy, dressed in a dirty, torn T-shirt and half-mast trousers, yet looking seriously confident in his job of indicating where the cars should park. A sharp burst of rain earlier on had left the soil a richer red colour and the 'car park' was pitted with deep puddles.

Elaborately dressed women and girls climbed out of vehicles and followed their suited menfolk across the vast expanse towards the sacred building. The tarmac road ran out just shy of the church, leaving the throng to pick their way in and out of the pockets of rain on the track leading to its door. The carless folk came too – straight-backed women walked proudly with their children following, their faces washed shiny and their short hair dust free and patted down neatly. It seemed to Ruth that there was no end to the people arriving.

The church service, which was announced for ten a.m., eventually began at something past eleven. Ruth could not tell exactly because her watch was playing up. It did not seem to matter anyway. None of these people looked as though they were in a hurry to rush back home for a Sunday roast. There was not enough room inside the building, and many people gathered outside in eager anticipation of what they were about to hear. Using a loud speaker, the minister addressed his flock, and they listened eagerly as he spoke.

In spite of the earlier rains, the atmosphere was still humid and Ruth felt pity for those standing outside where, she was sure, they would feel it more. She looked around. Every face was lifted, eyes focused towards the front of the church in great expectation. Throughout the service people called out, "Amen" or "Hallelujah" and the handkerchiefs were out in their droves, wiping faces and necks, whilst service sheets turned into fans. The fervent worship songs were joyous and energetic as though everyone was moving with the same pulse. No one stood still. Rich sat next to poor, everyone smiling and Ruth felt a great sense of unity in the room. She had thought, at first, it was some kind of brainwashing, but as she looked around, that was not the sense she was getting. People appeared to be fully present and engaged. They wanted to be there. Whatever her views on religion, this was clearly a hugely important part of their lives and one that they needed. This was survival. Ruth could not help thinking, though, it was also pageantry at its height.

***

In stark contrast to the morning, Ruth's afternoon began quietly, just as she wanted. She had been introduced to so many people before and after church and received so many invitations that her head was spinning. Naomi had invited her to lunch with them, but Ruth politely refused, saying she was still recovering from travelling and late nights. Naomi, who was used to Mzungus, accepted graciously.

Once alone again, Ruth wanted to think more about Doug and what to do with her new found realisation. She had no doubt that he was the object of her searching. How ironic that she had come all the way to Africa to get away from the torments of her life at home only to discover that he was here. One thing was for sure, she had to keep it from him that she knew, at least for the time being, until she figured out what to do.

Chapter 10

"But why do you have to rush off to Bukoba when you promised to come to this dinner I'm organising? I just don't understand you." Freja was not happy.

Andi's nonchalance was really eating her up. How could he not remember?

"You are a crazy girl," Andi laughed. "I said I would come but now I can't. It happens. We are not married."

It was not often Freja lost her cool on the outside but she was livid. She had gone to so much trouble to make sure Andi would be her guest at the DANIDA reception at the weekend. Some big names in the donor world were coming to Tanzania and her father was hosting them. Mwanza was on the schedule of visits and he had asked Freja to make sure they received a fitting welcome. She saw this as a great opportunity to put Andi in the spotlight as hers. It was the perfect chance to make sure that everyone, including Ruth, understood that he was taken.

"Can't you reschedule your trip?" Freja asked insistently.

Andi was becoming impatient. It was nine a.m. and his football team – Dar Dynos – was due to start a shift workers' training session at ten and he did not want to be late for this one. He was the team's top goal scorer this season and he had no intention of disappointing. He had made the best dining room in the hotel available for Freja's do. He had even hand-picked the best servers to wait on. What more did she want?

The donors' dinner was not really Andi's scene. He had only agreed to go because Freja had gone on and on at him that night, a few weeks ago, when they were enjoying themselves at the night club. He remembered he was really chilled after the Dynos had won their match, enjoying a few cans of Stella and full of expectation for the night ahead. Looking into those blue eyes and touching Freja's shapely, toned legs, he would have agreed to anything. The memory brought a smile to Andi's face, enraging Freja even more.

"I won't forgive you for this," she practically screamed.

Andi turned around, picked up his kit bag and calmly walked out of the hotel, raising his hand in a goodbye gesture to his receptionist as he did so. These Mzungus are something else, he thought.

***

Ruth and Naomi sat companionably at Naomi's desk in the sparsely furnished VSO office, drinking Bwana Rutiga's tea. As a child, Ruth's mum used condensed milk to make toffee. Drinking tea made with it was something of a novelty, but she welcomed its unusual sweetness that seemed to have a definite reviving effect.

"You know," said Naomi, flicking through the newly-prepared report, "instead of reading this, why don't I just show you what we do?"

"Sounds okay to me," Ruth responded.

"Yes, I think so. Let's go to Mkudi. You can see for yourself and get answers to your questions." Naomi hesitated, "Straight from the horse's nostril."

"I'm in your hands," Ruth said, suppressing a giggle.

"Sawa. Finish your chai and I will call Gilbert. Oh, and I advise you go to the toilet before we leave."

Strange thing to say to an adult, thought Ruth, though she took Naomi's advice nevertheless.

"Where's Doug?" Ruth asked when Naomi reappeared.

"He's gone out of town. We have a small project farther south along the lake shores and he's helping to dig pit latrines down there. He'll be gone for a couple of days."

Ruth was relieved. She felt apprehensive arriving at the office that morning, not knowing how she would react, seeing him again. Her plan was to divulge all in a phone call to her close friend, Isla, from the hotel that evening.

Gilbert headed north out of the city. Ruth recognised the long road that led to the airport. Naomi sat up front, the broken window to the side of her stuck halfway up. Along the way people called out to greet her, and she responded with her characteristic warmth and hearty laughter, at times straining to lean her head out of the window so as to finish off a conversation as Gilbert moved on with the crawling traffic.

Beads of sweat gathered along Ruth's hairline, every now and then dripping down along the contours of her face and neck. She was questioning what was the point of her shower that morning. Thankfully, she was dressed in loose wide-leg trousers and T-shirt. Her thick mane of red hair was gathered up into a high ponytail. Looking down at her feet, Ruth felt satisfied with her choice of dark blue, thick-soled plimsolls. She was learning.

Expertly directed by Gilbert, his vehicle began to climb a hill. They were ascending into Mkudi, one of the many overcrowded, unplanned settlements overlooking Mwanza city. The engine began to complain.

"Stop here, Gilbert," Naomi said, opening the door ready to climb down. Turning to Ruth, she continued, "We'll walk the rest of the way."

Smiling gratefully, Gilbert manoeuvred and began negotiating his way back down the slope.

They stood on a rocky path surrounded by makeshift dwellings. A stench filled the air. Ruth eyed her chaotic surroundings. Three women passed by carrying buckets on the crowns of their heads, each reaching a free hand up to steady their load as they picked a way through the rocks. Concentration prevented them from looking up. Not so the children who, gleefully and repeatedly, called out, "Mzungu! Mzungu! How are you?"

Ruth's cheerful response sent them into happy convulsions.

Pointing to the debris lining the manmade gulleys that ran alongside the houses, Naomi noted, "The rains have

59

set everything moving downhill. That will all end up in the lake."

Naomi was relieved that Ruth appeared to take everything in her stride with a generous respect. She remembered, with horror, the offence caused during Freja's first visit, when she had pulled an air freshener out of her pocket and proceeded to spray everything in her immediate vicinity.

Almost without exception everyone stared. As a youngster Ruth was taught it was rude to stare. She remembered feeling ashamed whenever she was caught doing it. There were no such inhibitions here. People just stared. Ruth was not upset or afraid. Rather she felt a need to connect, a need to show she was merely another person just like each of them. I'm really just like you inside, she wanted to tell them.

When Naomi exchanged words with passers-by, sometimes stopping for longer conversations, the children gathered round, holding onto each other as if for moral support whilst their eyes keenly followed the Mzungu with great curiosity.

"More than two-thirds of Mwanza's population lives like this," Naomi commented as they climbed higher, "with no access to clean water or proper sanitation."

"And the authorities, what are they doing?" Ruth asked.

"Not much. They have no money to run pipes up to these areas. Anything that gets done is initiated and orchestrated by community-based groups or international non-government organisations."

"So, how do people get water and sanitation?"

"Mostly, they go much farther down where there is a water tank. When that runs out, they go to the lake."

"And toilets?"

"There are some latrines also farther down that the council supposedly maintains. For that privilege people have to pay. If you can't pay – which is the case for many – you just go at the side of your hut. You can see and smell what happens to the waste."

Ruth kept quiet. Anything she said would be incongruous in the circumstances.

The women continued, up along a bumpy path running through the middle of two rows of huts. The roofs were flat, constructed from plastic sheeting, corrugated iron and other materials that Ruth was unable to identify. The walls of the huts were sealed with mud that had turned to clay in the baking sun. Open spaces served as a door and a window. Thin pieces of material draped down over the spaces provided the only privacy.

There were women bending over metal pots on open fires, stirring their contents, other women washing cooking utensils, young boys and girls scrubbing clothes in dirty water held in colourful plastic buckets whilst very small children sat on the ground playing quietly with a shoe, a plastic container or some other object they picked up from outside the hut.

It was extremely hot, and with no shade Ruth's head began to ache. She did not want to wear sunglasses because she felt they would create distance between her and the people she was amongst. But her green eyes were not made for the intensity of the African sun. Just as Ruth considered putting her glasses on, Naomi pointed ahead. "That's the house we are visiting today," she said.

Looking up, Ruth could see the odd tree punctuating the skyline beyond them behind the last crooked row of dwellings. Turning around, she glanced back downhill. The settlement was alive with people, all of them busy doing something and yet there was none of the sense of urgency she felt in Mwanza city. She had not been in Africa long enough to understand, she knew that. But at that moment, arriving there for the first time, she felt a sense of resignation in the rhythm of the people as they went about their daily chores.

A teenage girl came out of the home in front of them. Dressed in a grubby kitenge, her feet bare, she greeted Naomi respectfully, "Shikamoo". There was no excitement about her, just quiet humility.

Naomi responded. Then she introduced Ruth, who – not knowing what else to do – went to shake the girl's unresponsive hand.

"This is Rwehema," Naomi said. "She lives here with her four younger siblings."

Rwehema indicated for Naomi and Ruth to follow her inside and they did so, the sudden darkness taking a few seconds to adjust to.

Four children sat on the ground looking intently at their visitors. Ruth and Naomi sat down opposite them when invited. Naomi chatted easily with the children who responded shyly, barely a smile between them. Rwehema looked tired and moved lethargically. The ground was bare. There was just one room. Ruth could see what looked like a rolled-up mat leaning against the wall in one corner of that room and in the other a few tin plates and mugs, a red plastic bowl and a green bucket. The clothes the children were wearing were torn and dirty and their legs, feet, arms and hands were a greyish colour just as Ruth had seen on the street children in the town centre and the boy who grabbed hold of her case at the airport.

That day in Mkudi, five pairs of bewildered, tired eyes reached into Ruth's soul, leaving a deep, indescribable impression.

Chapter 11

"The girl is fifteen, Isla, fifteen!"

Back at the hotel, Ruth spoke passionately down the phone line. "Her parents are dead. She has no job, no grandparents or aunties and uncles and four younger ones to look after." There was silence on the line. "Naomi – my boss – told me some men have been hanging around her place at night. She is frightened and vulnerable and she doesn't look at all well."

The two friends talked, Isla asking questions about what help was available, Ruth trying to explain the difficulties faced by those who want to help. "Naomi says there are many more like her, thousands even!" Ruth understood that it was hard for Isla to appreciate the true situation. Only a week ago the two of them were the same, not giving a thought to what was happening on the other side of the world unless their attention was caught by a brief item on the news or such like. Why should they? Their lives were busy and full and they had problems of their own. Plus, there were plenty of people in need where they lived.

With her immediate thoughts and feelings about the situation in Mkudi exhausted, Ruth turned her attention to other matters.

"I need you to do something for me," she told Isla. "I need you to get hold of that newspaper article, the one I showed you ages ago, that came out when Rachel was killed. You mustn't breathe a word to anyone but the guy who did it is here."

Before they could talk more the line went dead, leaving Ruth contemplating the full implications of what she had just spoken aloud. Feeling overwhelmed, she decided to go down to the bar for a drink.

"Hey, stranger." Andi called over to her as she walked through the glass doors to the bar area. In total contrast to her mood, he was looking very cheerful. "Jambo! Habari?" he said, approaching her enthusiastically.

Trying to smile, Ruth greeted him back saying she was fine, though he did not appear convinced.

"Come and join me. I'm just finishing up then we can have some time to talk together."

Not knowing whether it was Andi's company she wanted, she reluctantly agreed, feeling it would be rude to refuse. "You seem very happy tonight," she said.

"Yes, my team is playing really well. We had a great training session this morning. We are definitely ready to take on the Mighty Simbas tomorrow night. That makes me happy."

"I'm glad to hear that," Ruth said, trying to sound upbeat.

"You, on the other hand, seem not so happy," Andi commented.

"Oh, I'm okay."

"Well, that's not very convincing. Tell me, what's wrong?"

"Do you mind if we don't talk about it? I just need to forget…"

Before she could continue, Andi jumped out of his chair and made a beeline for the bar. "I have the perfect remedy," he said, reaching for a tall, brown brandy bottle standing on the top shelf behind the bar. "Another one of Andi's perfect mixes. You will soon feel better," he grinned.

As she drank, Ruth began to relax. She could feel herself letting go. The two of them chatted and laughed about all sorts of things. She noticed Andi was only drinking fruit juices and asked him why.

"I need to be great tomorrow," he said. "We are going to win but not if I get drunk tonight."

It didn't matter to Ruth, she was enjoying herself and began to feel carefree for the first time in a week. Andi was very attentive and seemed even more attractive than she had thought. She was finding it hard to pull her eyes away from his and even found herself affectionately touching his arm or his leg as she chatted. Every time Ruth emptied her glass, Andi jumped up to make her another one of his concoctions, telling her she could be his "guinea fowl" to try out his new ideas.

"Don't you mean guinea pig?" Ruth laughed gently.

Andi looked puzzled, smiled and carried on mixing and pouring.

"Andi, you are really handsome, you know. I bet you have to fight the girls off," Ruth said, touching his face with her hand.

A little surprised – Andi had not had Ruth down as such a confident, flirty type – he took his opportunity nonetheless. "Well you, Miss Ruth, are a beautiful woman. I told you that before but you didn't believe me. I bet *you* have to fight the boys away," he responded.

Ruth threw her head back and laughed, a full belly laugh that felt really good.

"You should not laugh," Andi smiled. His voice was deep and seductive, and Ruth was falling quickly under his spell. He guided her face towards his, looked her straight in the eyes and said, "Ruth Ross, you are a beautiful lady. Believe it." Then he leaned in towards her and kissed her softly and gently on the forehead.

"Is that it?" Ruth asked, still smiling.

"For now," Andi said with a wink.

***

The next day Andi woke with the sun. He felt light and ready to conquer the world. There was no hangover and no fatigue, just the memory of a night spent seducing Ruth Ross. It had been much easier than he thought it would be and he felt proud of his achievement. Besides, there was something about Ruth. He couldn't quite put a name to it but he liked it nevertheless.

Being in the habit of using one of the spare hotel rooms if he was particularly late or had to be there

67

especially early in a morning, smuggling Ruth into one of them the night before had been easy for Andi. He made sure, though, that he escorted her back to her own room before daylight, saying he was 'protecting her honour' and keeping his spotless record as an assistant manager. That had given him another couple of hours sleep, and now he knew he would play well in the evening.

The light on Andi's cell phone was flashing. He turned over and picked it up from the bedside table. He had a voice message. He dialled his voicemail and listened.

"Andwele Bwana, we are so excited to see you. Kemi keeps asking, 'When is Daddy coming?' I can't wait to hear how the plans are going. We'll talk at the weekend. Love you."

Andi turned back to lie flat. He smiled, closed his eyes and pictured his little girl holding her arms out to him. He would have to bring her something special from Mwanza. Her mother would expect it. Another thing to do before Friday. But first his shift and tonight's football match...

Chapter 12

On Tuesday morning, Ruth arrived in the office feeling a little worse for wear and a little like everyone she spoke to could see right into her and knew what she had been up to the night before. Things were a bit of a blur but there was no mistaking the fact that she had spent the night with Andi. Part of her felt ashamed of her behaviour, especially after such a short time in the country, but she was glowing inside and she could not ignore that. Andi was such a gentleman, so charming and attentive. What a catch! 'Oh no, what about Freja?' Ruth thought. They would just have to be diplomatic about their relationship and let Freja down gently. After all, Freja could have her pick of guys. She would not miss Andi.

"Sawa, but this weekend doesn't leave much time to get things ready." Naomi was talking to Salvatore on the phone and indicated to Ruth to take a seat.

"Yes, I do realise the house won't build itself. Your cousins need paying, yes. Yes, I know, you haven't been there for ages. You're taking Julius and Andi with you? Good, I feel better about that. See you at home later."

Naomi smiled at Ruth. "Unamkaji?"

Feeling a little awkward in Naomi's presence, Ruth smiled and said she had slept well and was looking forward to the day ahead.

"Sawa. Now, I want to tell you about my idea for Rwehema. Freja, please ask Bwana Rutiga to bring us all chai."

Flustered, Ruth turned around to see Freja at the other end of the room and greeted her nervously, a greeting that was met with the indifference Ruth had come to expect. Diverting her eyes, Ruth tried to concentrate on what Naomi was explaining.

"I am very concerned for Rwehema's safety. I think it's imperative we get her out of that isolated situation where she is too vulnerable."

"How do you propose to do that?" Freja asked.

"Because of the urgency of the situation, I want to speak to another family living a bit farther down. There are three teenage boys and a father. I'm going to ask them to do a swap.

"Do you think they will agree to move further away from toilets and a water source?" Ruth enquired.

"I don't know but they are young and reasonably fit. No one in the family is ill. I am confident they will go for it."

In her heart Naomi knew a small financial incentive might be needed, but she didn't want to divulge her thoughts on that. It would have to be a private arrangement, not for Freja, Ruth or anyone else to worry about.

"I propose we go back today and sort this out."

"What happens if they don't agree?" Freja was persistent.

"We'll come to that bridge when we cross it," Naomi replied, momentarily disturbing Ruth's serious countenance.

Freja was not at all keen to accompany Naomi and Ruth.

"I have a lot to organise here for Friday night's dinner. I will stay behind and get on with that," she said. Usually it was Naomi who gave the orders, but she could hardly refuse when future funding might depend on the success or otherwise of Freja's event. If truth be told, she was even a bit relieved to be going just with Ruth, who she had noticed was especially quiet. It would give them a chance to talk more. Besides, she would not have to worry about any insensitive behaviour in a potentially delicate situation.

An hour later, leaving Freja to put the finishing touches to her name place cards for the tables, Naomi and Ruth pulled out of the courtyard in Naomi's pickup, heading north to Mkudi.

***

Alone in the office, Freja reflected on Ruth's earlier demeanour. There was something different about her; Freja could sense it.

The telephone rang. "VSO Mwanza," Freja answered.

"How are the preparations for Friday going?"

It was her father. Before she could answer, he went on.

71

"Remember, this has to go well. I've had some disappointing feedback about you, young lady. This is your chance to redeem yourself."

Naomi and her big mouth, thought Freja.

"Everything will be fine, Dad. You'll see," she said.

"It had better be. I can't guarantee your allowance will continue if this doesn't bring results."

Technically, Freja's father could not send her home, but there was no way she could stay in Africa without his money. Having dropped out of university, she had nothing to go back to and her mother would never let her hear the end of it.

Freja looked at her list of acceptances and continued working on the name cards. Yesterday Andi had made her mad, but she needed him on board if her evening was to be a success. She resolved to go and see him before he went off shift. But first, those cards had to be finished.

***

Arriving at Mkudi, Naomi and Ruth were greeted by a worrying sight. A procession of young and old was making its way silently and slowly down the hill towards them.

"This is not good," said Naomi. "Something very bad has happened. I feel it."

The women watched anxiously as the human train came closer and closer. Then the wailing began, growing louder and louder with each approaching step.

As the people neared them, Ruth could see that four men close to the front of the line carried a stretcher covered over with a colourful kanga. Four pairs of frightened eyes followed behind. Naomi gasped with the sudden realisation that the body underneath the cloth was Rwehema's.

Chapter 13

The culprit was malaria. After weeks of illness, with no prospect of medical attention, Rwehema's temperature had soared in the night. She was too ill and too poor to go anywhere for help and no ambulance could make it up to her dwelling. The oldest sibling had run to a neighbour but it was too late. Another life lost to a perfectly treatable condition.

In silence, Naomi drove the children back to town to the Catholic hostel for orphans where she spoke to the nun-in-charge, leaving her with money to buy food, clothes and a medical check-up. She promised to return in a month's time.

"They could not have stayed alone in Mkudi," Naomi said aloud on the drive back to the Ramada hotel. It had been a long, tiring day. Both women were emotionally and physically exhausted. Naomi admired the way Ruth took time to think, comfortable with silence, not feeling as though it had to be filled.

Approaching the front entrance, they saw Andi rushing out, his kitbag in hand.

"Am I glad to see you! Can you drop me at the stadium, Mom, please?"

Naomi agreed.

Seeing Ruth, Andi said, "Come along and watch. It's going to be a great match."

"Let's go, Ruth," Naomi said. "It will do us good and help us think about something else for a while."

Ruth agreed, though she was not convinced it would wipe the day's events from her mind.

"I'm glad your father persuaded you and Julius to go with him at the weekend," Naomi said as she turned the vehicle back around.

"Yes, I am looking forward to it. It'll give me a chance to catch up with some old friends too," Andi responded cheerfully.

Ruth, who was sitting up front, had her back to Andi and could not see the expression on his face but there was no mistaking his hand as it reached around the side of her seat to pat her leg, making her giggle. Naomi glanced across to see what Ruth was laughing at. If these two young people thought Naomi had not noticed the chemistry flying between them, she would leave them to their illusion.

The match was great fun to watch. The Dar Dynos won deservedly with a score of two-one. Andi scored both goals. He seemed to flit about as light as a feather and strike with demon accuracy when he executed both shots. Ruth remembered the last football match she attended, standing in the freezing cold, donning bobble hat and gloves and stamping her feet whilst her dad shouted excitedly at his team. What a contrast to the balmy evening heat at the Mwanza Sports Club's floodlit pitch.

Sitting in Naomi's vehicle after the match, the women talked about their day.

"If only I had acted yesterday when we went to see her," Naomi lamented.

"You couldn't have known what was going to happen." Ruth tried to offer some consolation.

"Rwehema's death should not have happened. We need to do an urgent sweep of Mkudi to identify the most vulnerable families."

Ruth understood Naomi's passionate response to the day's tragedy, but she feared that the resources of one small NGO were not enough to tackle the sheer scale of the problems facing Mkudi and many other wards like it. Of course, Naomi knew that better than her.

"I need to put something compelling together for Friday night to hand to donor representatives. We can't let this opportunity go." Naomi's tone was urgent, and Ruth agreed to help prepare a strategy document.

"By the way, where is Andi?" asked Ruth. "It's been almost an hour since the match ended."

Naomi laughed. "Oh, he's a big celebrity now and celebrities have free license to keep people waiting," she said.

When they eventually reached the Ramada again, Naomi dropped her two passengers off and drove away, leaving Ruth and Andi standing together on the hotel steps. She watched them closely in her cracked rear-view mirror as they grew smaller and smaller and eventually disappeared from sight.

Tired and badly in need of a shower, Ruth made her excuses and headed straight inside for the lift.

"Where are you going?" Andi called after her.

"It's been a long day," Ruth replied.

"Oh no! You don't get away that easily. We are going to celebrate the Dynos' win today. Make sure you are back here in fifteen minutes or I will come and get you." Andi smiled and winked.

Acknowledging him with a wave of her hand, Ruth disappeared into the open lift doors.

Still grinning, Andi turned around and came face to face with a not-too-happy-looking Freja.

"I've been waiting for you," she said accusingly.

"And I've been playing football," Andi retorted indignantly.

"It looks like it," Freja said, nodding towards the lift where Ruth had been standing.

Andi did not have time for this. "What do you want Freja?"

Freja was fuming, again. What did she want? This Ruth person has been in Mwanza for less than a week, and suddenly Freja is the outsider. Oh no! That wasn't happening. But she had to be clever.

"Oh, Andi, take no notice of me. I'm stressed with all the organising. Come, let me buy you a drink. I heard you say you won. Did you score? Tell me all about it."

Ruth took longer than fifteen minutes but no Andi appeared at her door, so she made her way downstairs. She had made an effort to look nice but was trying to make it look like she had not. She was not prepared to see Andi and Freja all cosied up in the bar, laughing and talking together. She turned to go back upstairs but hesitated.

"Hey, come back!" Andi called. "Come and join us. What do you want to drink?"

Roles reversed, Ruth did not feel like drinking after the night before. Reluctantly she sat in the seat Andi pulled up for her, meeting Freja's cold stare as she did so. Andi jumped up to get the juice she requested whilst Freja made no attempt whatsoever to make conversation. Instead, she drank to keep up with Andi, and she chatted and laughed to make herself more amenable to him and hopefully more interesting than Ruth who sat barely saying a word.

Ruth was beginning to plan her escape when who should walk into the bar but Doug, accompanied by a very tall, striking woman.

"Hey, guys. How have you been?"

Doug's companion smiled broadly and greeted each of them individually. It was clear to Ruth she had met Andi and Freja before. A rich smell of coconut wafted up Ruth's nose as Khadeja leaned in to take her hand. Bright red lipstick accentuated her full mouth and an off-the-shoulder white mini dress and thick gold arm bangle contrasted perfectly with her dark, lustrous skin.

Ruth was in no mood to tolerate Doug, who was clearly on a high, especially in the presence of his woman. In different circumstances she might have been tempted to tell him what she knew but instead she was beginning to feel like a fifth wheel.

"I thought you were gone for a few days," she said, sounding a little more disgruntled than she had meant to.

Doug was taken aback. "Well, it didn't work out that way. I will be going back next week," he said curtly.

Unable to stomach the situation any longer, Ruth got up, "I'm sorry, people, but I really need to sleep," she said as she turned and made her way back towards the lift, leaving three people bewildered and one absolutely delighted.

Chapter 14

Salvatore was excited about his forthcoming trip. He sat at his kitchen table making a 'Things to do' list – something he had been introduced to by a Canadian colleague. It was not going well. So far he had one thing on there – 'purchase ferry tickets'.

"It's a shame we could not fly," he said aloud.

"Mm," his wife agreed. "Still, it will mean you can spend more on the house."

Naomi was distracted. She and Ruth had three days to put a presentation together and make final preparations for Friday night. How was she going to persuade a bunch of Mzungu men to part with their ever-decreasing budgets? She had better come up with something good.

"Hodi!" Julius' voice called out through the open door.

"Karibu!" His parents welcomed him in unison.

Without hesitation, Naomi shifted into mother mode. "Sit, sit. Habari za siku? How has your day been? Do you want some food?"

Julius entered the kitchen and poked his nose into the pot sitting on top of the stove. "Mmm, smells good," he said approvingly. "I will have some of that but just a little. Gloria says I need to go on a diet," he laughed, patting his belly.

"Play football with your brother. You always used to," Salvatore pitched in.

"You know how it is when you're a lawyer, Dad. Not much time for that. But I do miss it. Maybe when we get back from Bukoba I should," Julius said unconvincingly.

After they had eaten, Naomi suggested they all drive to the Ramada where the boys could help Salvatore plan for the trip and she and Ruth could set out their own agenda for the donors' gathering.

At the hotel, Naomi was disappointed to see Andi and Freja sitting so closely together in a corner and a little surprised to see Doug and Khadeja. Andi's keenness to be separate from Freja when his parents walked in was not lost on his mother, nor on Freja.

Naomi greeted Doug first then the other three before enquiring after Ruth.

"Oh, she's gone to sleep," Freja said cheerfully.

Naomi was doubtful. She read the situation straight away and felt that Ruth would not be sleeping at eight p.m. Nevertheless, she decided to call the room to be sure.

"Hello, Ruth, we are here with Salva and Julius. The boys are talking about their trip, so I thought we could have a chat if you are not too tired."

"I would love that." Ruth jumped up from where she was dozing. "Give me a minute and I'll be down."

Naomi relocated to another corner of the bar and ordered two coffees. When Ruth appeared, Naomi was concerned to see her eyes were red and slightly puffy.

"My dear, are you all right? You don't have to tell me but if you want to…"

There was a loud thud. Naomi and Ruth turned to see Freja knocking over a chair in her rush to leave the building, a look of anger on her face. Naomi turned back, smiled knowingly at Ruth then continued.

"As I was saying, don't be afraid to speak out if something is bothering you, my dear. We are here to help."

There was something about the look on Naomi's face that made Ruth feel reassured and she started offloading. Once started, she could not stop. She talked of her discovery about Doug and her plans to expose him. She told Naomi about her growing feelings for Andi and her confusion over his relationship with Freja. Through it all Naomi said nothing, just looked at her, from time to time holding her hand. She spoke only when she was sure Ruth had finished.

"You must be very shocked to find Doug in this place, especially when you came here to get away from your problems at home."

Ruth nodded and a lone tear found its way down her cheek and fell into the sodden tissue she was squeezing with both hands.

"Clearly I did not know this about Doug. It is a very sad thing," Naomi continued. "I can only say that since he has been here in Mwanza he has been a great help to many people. I am not sure where I would be without his help."

Naomi hesitated, knowing what she was saying would be difficult for Ruth to hear. "I think that maybe this thing that happened a long time ago when Doug was young and restless has played a part in making him the person he is now, who spends his time helping others." Another hesitation. "I cannot tell you what to do but my advice is for you to try to find it in your heart to forgive or maybe to let sleeping cats lie down. To drag everything up again will only bring pain to you, your parents and Doug."

Ruth had never, ever considered forgiveness as an option. Sitting there opposite Naomi, listening to her speak, steadily and sincerely, Ruth began to wonder.

"Doug has not got away completely unpunished. He banished himself from his family, his home and everything he knew. There must have been pain for him too."

Ruth was shocked. Suddenly she was meant to feel sorry for Doug! That was not happening.

"You know, my dear, you might find it releases you to move on with your life whilst still keeping the memory of your sister alive."

Caught out by Naomi's suggestion, Ruth wondered, could she really let herself do this?

"As for my son, Andi, he is young and the affection of pretty girls turns his head, I am afraid. Have patience. He is a good boy at heart."

Ruth felt embarrassed. She doubted the wisdom of telling a man's mother how she felt and she began to steer the conversation in another direction, just as Salvatore, Julius and Andi came to join them.

"We have decided to travel on Friday," Salvatore announced to his wife. "There's a ferry that leaves around midday."

"So, there's much to do before then," Naomi replied with a complicit smile aimed at Ruth.

Chapter 15

"I've had an idea," Ruth announced to Naomi in the VSO office on Wednesday morning. "Why don't we get Rwehema's younger brother and sisters to speak at the dinner on Friday night? That way the donors will hear their story first-hand. It should make more of an impression."

Naomi thought. "You know, I think that is an excellent idea, if they agree. We will go and visit them today and talk to them about it."

Excited with their plans, Ruth and Naomi began to map out how they thought the presentation should go and what visual aids and equipment they would need.

The sweet tea Bwana Rutiga brought them was welcomed enthusiastically. Speaking in Kihaya, he handed Naomi a piece of folded paper and pointed to the legs of her desk. Taking the paper, Naomi nodded approvingly. She explained to Ruth that Doug had been in and shaved a section off the legs to make them equal and the table steady. She placed the folded paper in her bag, and they both laughed.

Freja telephoned the office to say she was busy at the hotel, finalising the catering order. Naomi felt sure Freja was avoiding her but did not mind. She and Ruth needed to get this presentation right and it was easier with Freja out of the way. Still, if VSO come out of this event with additional funding, Naomi knew she would have to acknowledge Freja's efforts in putting the whole thing together. She had never known Freja to work so hard.

Out of the window, Ruth could see Doug pacing up and down in the courtyard, his cell phone raised to his ear. She could not hear what he said but, judging by the look on his face, he was not happy at all. The idea that he might be having some difficulties was strangely comforting to Ruth as she turned her focus back to their plans.

Later that day, Ruth and Naomi pulled up outside the Catholic orphanage once again. They were greeted warmly by one of the sisters who took them to the visitors' lounge. It was heartening to see Rwehema's siblings washed and dressed in clean clothes but they were clearly still bewildered and very sad.

"They have insisted on being together at all times," the sister said.

"Well, it is very early," Naomi responded. "Perhaps given time they might relax a bit. Let me talk to them."

"Go ahead. I will bring some chai."

The sister vacated the room, leaving Ruth and Naomi facing the four children who stood up straight, holding on to each other. Naomi approached them and greeted each one gently and as she did so they each let go to give her a hug.

Naomi invited everyone to sit, the children in a line on a low sofa opposite her and Ruth. She leaned forward and began to speak in a low, soothing tone. She asked the children how they were feeling and what they understood of what was happening to them and what they wanted to

85

happen. Slowly, the two older children began to open up, responding to Naomi's warmth. They told her that they felt very sad about their sister, Rwehema, but they felt lucky to be at the orphanage with food and clothes and people to care for them. The older boy, Manzi, said the thing he wanted most was for him and his sisters to go to school. He said he knew it was the only chance they had to change their situation and eventually go back to Mkudi to help others there.

Naomi explained about her work in simple terms. She told the children about the meeting on Friday night and she asked Manzi if he would help her to help him do just what he had said he wanted. Manzi agreed. He looked at his sister, Byera, who nodded. The younger two simply sat and stared.

Ruth and Naomi were served with tea which they drank whilst the children were taken outside where others were playing. Ruth caught up with what had been discussed.

"They are very tentative but Manzi can speak well," Naomi told her. "Of course, I will need to translate but hopefully just seeing his expressions will help. At least it is worth a try."

Naomi left instructions with the sisters to have Manzi and Byera picked up on Friday afternoon. Then she and Ruth drove away as the children stood waving.

"They will be okay," Naomi said as they pulled onto the main road. "God will see to that."

Ruth said nothing.

Chapter 16

It was Friday morning. Doug sat out on his veranda, such as it was, drinking coffee that Khadeja had made him and trying to understand how he had got himself into the scrape he was in. He heard his cell phone go off inside and Khadeja answer it. He wished she would not do that. He could not count how many times he had asked her – even told her – not to. But Khadeja did not trust any man and told him, matter-of-factly, if he wanted her in his life, she would carry on doing it.

"Dougee, Dougee, it's Christopher." Khadeja appeared in the doorway, holding the phone out to him.

Doug's heart sank as he took the handset. "Christopher," he said, "what can I do for you?"

"You haven't forgotten you owe me, have you, Dougee?" Christopher pronounced Doug's name just as Khadeja had done, in jest.

"How could I? You keep reminding me."

"I can't wait forever. It would be such a pity if anything happened to spoil that beautiful face." Christopher was referring to Khadeja and Doug knew it.

"I'll sort it. Just give me until after the weekend."

"Last chance, Dougee, last chance."

The line went dead.

"What will you sort, Dougee?" Khadeja had been listening.

"Oh, just some job he wants me to do. I've been promising for a while."

Unconvinced, Khadeja decided to let it go for the time being. She would get to the bottom of it later.

***

For the first time, Ruth found herself alone in the office. Naomi was running around doing last-minute shopping for Salvatore's trip. Thursday had been really busy. Freja was occupied with decorating the dining room at the hotel and giving instructions to the staff that would be waiting on. There were still signs to be made, tables to set out and technical equipment to set up and test.

Ruth was busy making back-up visual aids in case of a power failure that might prevent them playing her PowerPoint presentation. She and Andi had managed to squeeze in a drink together at the end of the evening. He told her he would not be gone long and on his return they would have lots more time together. She had not minded; she was tired and her mind was full of Friday evening.

Naturally, Naomi would be going to the ferry terminal to see the men off. Ruth and Gilbert were charged with picking up Manzi and Byera and taking them to get smart new outfits in town before the evening do.

"Take them for ice cream too," Naomi said. "It will be a good treat for them."

***

At seven-thirty p.m. Ruth stood in the foyer of the Ramada hotel with Manzi and Byera on either side of her and Naomi ahead. As the delegates arrived, they were greeted and shown to their seats. Everyone looked very smart. Even Freja had managed to select a suitably conservative outfit that befitted the occasion. Ruth watched Freja as she strutted around, speaking with ease in her Danish mother tongue to the guests who clearly found her very charming. One man seemed particularly familiar with her and obviously knew Naomi too. Ruth supposed it was Freja's father, but he was not introduced to her.

The children looked great. Manzi in long trousers, blazer, white shirt and dark red tie, and Byera in a simple loose pink satin-look dress with white ankle socks and shiny black shoes. Their cropped hair was clean, combed and patted down with oil and their skin showed no sign of its former greyness. Ruth could tell they were both nervous but she was proud of their composure in such an unfamiliar setting.

Naomi cut a stunning figure in her traditional dress and matching headscarf. She certainly commanded the attention of every eye when she got up to address the room. She spoke in English as it was the common language for everyone except the children. She was clear and authoritative as she summarised the VSO projects in and around Mwanza over the past two years and highlighted the challenges faced, without reservation. Finally, she introduced the children.

"We felt it was important to give these children a voice," she said. "They do not only speak for themselves but for thousands of others like them who face the daily realities of life in our slums."

Manzi and Byera walked hesitantly onto the platform to join Naomi. Handing them a microphone each, she began to ask questions and translate them, as well as the children's answers, to the audience. She invited questions from the floor and translated those for the children to answer. Manzi and Byera spoke slowly and deliberately with a simple honesty. Ruth looked around her. Everyone was listening.

When the interviewing was over, the visitors stood up and clapped. The children's eyes flitted in awe from one delegate to another. Ruth knew it was quite overwhelming for them but, like Naomi, she felt it would make a big difference to the outcome of the evening.

A sister from the orphanage arrived, with Gilbert, to escort the children back home. Ruth accompanied them outside and promised to visit soon. Giving them both a hug, she said her goodbyes and returned to her seat.

Before stepping down, Naomi played tribute to Freja who responded with delight, basking in the words of praise which, Ruth had to admit, were well-deserved. Then it was Freja's father's turn. As the Danish country representative in Tanzania, he spoke on behalf of DANIDA. He was clearly impressed with Naomi and the children. He even praised the PowerPoint, making Ruth blush, though no one saw. But most importantly, he announced that, subject to detailed proposals and budgets, DANIDA was committed to providing additional funding over the coming five-year period. Naomi glanced over at Ruth and smiled. Ruth smiled back. Their hard work had paid off.

People started to fidget in their seats. They must be hungry, thought Ruth. Just one last part to sit through – journalists' questions.

Sitting along the back of the room, the journalists had been invited for the presentation. It was important they print/broadcast the verbal commitment made by the Danes to additional funding as soon as possible, and they would be returning soon to their respective offices to do just that. One man stood up and took the roving microphone.

"Stephen Rweyamamu, Daily News," he announced. "Most of the people living in these unplanned settlements have come from Kagera region on the other side of Lake Victoria looking for work."

There were nods of agreement around the room.

"My question is, will there be any money for improving the ferry services so we don't have to keep experiencing disasters like today's?"

"Today's?" Naomi and Ruth turned sharply, looking enquiringly at the speaker.

"You haven't heard?" he said. "The midday ferry capsized halfway across the lake. All seven hundred passengers are missing, presumed drowned."

Chapter 17

At precisely nine-thirty-five p.m. on Friday, Naomi's world stopped. She had no idea what happened before or after that. She did not know how she got home from the donors' dinner or how Ruth came to be in her house with her. She did not even remember moving from her bedroom to the lounge where she was sitting, wrapped in a Kanga, staring at the white wall in front of her.

Ruth knelt on the floor at Naomi's feet. Taking her hands, she whispered, "I am so sorry."

Naomi looked at her blankly. Seeing the concern in Ruth's eyes, she remembered.

Naomi's eyes closed. She tried to think but her mind would not focus. A sharp ache swirled around her stomach and wound itself up towards her throat, causing her to let out a gasp. She opened her eyes. Ruth was still kneeling in the same position. Although she was unable to move, Naomi knew that Ruth being there was a good thing. It stopped her from falling over the edge of the cliff she was so desperately clinging on to.

Ruth did not know how long the two of them sat like that. She did not hear the door nor Gloria silently moving across the floor, bending down and placing her own hands over theirs. Her head, covered with a scarf, bent low, tears falling silently, dropping one after the other onto Ruth's hands.

Each woman had her own grief. Ruth knew, though, that Naomi's was the greatest loss. How she would ever recover from losing her entire family in one go, Ruth had no idea. There were no words, so they sat, just as they were, with their own thoughts. Suddenly Naomi lifted her head and with frightened eyes she urged, "Pray with me. If ever I needed God, it's now," she whispered. Holding hands and united in their grief, the women prayed like they had never prayed before.

The days following the accident passed in a blur. Ruth and Gloria took it in turns to make sure Naomi was not alone at any time. At first, scores of visitors came by the house to pay their respects and there was much wailing. Naomi received them all humbly, without saying much, retreating to her room to pray as soon as they left. Ruth and Gloria spent their time trying to come to terms with the situation and preparing meals.

"You need to eat," they told Naomi who responded as if on auto pilot.

The house remained largely silent, with the exception of when visitors came by. With the passing days and no news of bodies being retrieved, the visitors began to trail off. Gloria told Ruth they were afraid and suspicious because no one knew where the bodies were and so they could not be sure they were really dead. Gloria was unfocussed and incapable of arranging anything and Ruth did not understand the traditions and how to follow them. It seemed that the only surviving male relatives were in

Bukoba, and they would be afraid to make the trip across the lake, Ruth was sure of that.

One day Gloria announced that she was going home to her parents. "I need to start again," she said. "I have nothing left."

Ruth understood but wondered how she would manage Naomi without her. The only thing she was sure of was that she would not abandon her.

Naomi, who had no interest in anything, begged Ruth to go too. "You are young. You need to get on with your life," she said. "I will be okay in time."

"I am not leaving you," Ruth replied. "And, besides, I need to tell you that I am having Andi's baby – your grandchild."

For the first time since that fateful day, Naomi cried properly. She cried like she had never cried before and she could not stop. She cried so much she had to gasp for air in between her sobs. Ruth stayed close but quiet. Unsure what the crying meant, she waited. Eventually Naomi's body stopped shaking, her tears stopped rolling and she lifted her face towards Ruth.

"This is a miracle," she said. "Don't you see, God has made Andi live on. Andwele means 'a gift from God'. This baby is truly a gift from God."

Relieved, yet worried, Ruth held Naomi's hands once again. "So, you see, I can't leave now. This child needs you as much as it needs me," she said.

Naomi smiled weakly. "We will look after each other," she replied.

Chapter 18

Like everyone, Doug was shocked by what had happened. He liked Naomi's family and was used to being around them. But now his dilemma was becoming worse. He had not been able to keep his word to Christopher, and in fear of repercussions on Khadeja, he had persuaded her to go to Dodoma to spend time with her sister and family. He had given her what little money he had left and drove her to the bus park. He knew her and wanted to make sure she actually left town. He could not risk her finding out what he was planning next.

Doug rarely thought back to his reasons for coming to Mwanza in the first place. It had been difficult at first, but a few years in, the terrible image of a little girl's frightened eyes just before his car hit her, began to fade until the day when he did not think of her at all, not once for a whole day.

Rummaging around in his underwear drawer, he located the delicately folded newspaper and pulled it out. Carefully he unfolded it. A friend of his had sent Doug the clipping which appeared in the Dumfries Gazette at the time of the incident. It reported 'Young Girl Dies After Hit and Run.' When he received it, Doug knew he could never go back to Scotland. Reading past the headline, Doug's attention was caught anew by the detail in the article. The girl's name was Rachel Ross and she was survived by a sister, Ruth, and parents, Anthony and Anita. Thoughtfully, Doug folded the newspaper article for the umpteenth time and replaced it at the back of the drawer from where he had taken it. It was no use dwelling on that, he told himself. His priority now was planning his next move.

***

Ruth decided to check out of the Ramada. It seemed to make sense as she only had a few things left in her room and she was spending most of her time at Naomi's place.

"A hotel is no place for a pregnant woman," Naomi said.

Ruth was glad. Being there only reminded her of Andi, and besides, why should VSO be paying for a room when she was barely in it? Her clothes and other personal items packed, Ruth made her way downstairs in the lift. Gilbert came to escort her to Naomi's. Driving through Mwanza, they passed Freja walking, head high, one arm linked with a young attractive male dressed in suit and tie. She looks happy, at least, thought Ruth cynically.

***

It was midnight as Doug approached Naomi's bungalow on foot. He had left his vehicle some way away, so as not to draw attention. Naomi's security guard was nowhere to be seen, just as Doug planned. One of his contacts had taken a payment in exchange for distracting the guard. Doug would have no more than twenty minutes to get in and out of Naomi's house. Knowing the house and its contents, Doug could be pretty targeted. He would be the last person Naomi would suspect. He would pay off his debt, get Khadeja back and then go back to a peaceful life and Naomi would be none the wiser.

Inside the bungalow, things were going well for Doug. He managed to grab a few items of value and stick them into the drawstring sports bag that he had swung over one shoulder. Five minutes left. Doug walked across the sitting room floor in his stockinged feet. One more item and he knew exactly what it was and where to find it.

"Doug!"

Doug nearly jumped out of his skin. Right up in his face was Ruth's.

"Doug! What on earth are you doing here?" Ruth exclaimed.

In his panic, Doug turned and slipped on the polished floor, dropping his bag and waking Naomi with a loud thud as all six foot of him came crashing down to the ground, banging his head on the edge of the low table as he did so.

When a blurry-eyed Naomi entered the room, she saw Ruth standing over a stunned Doug, shaking her finger in his face and shouting, "You won't get away with it this time! Call the police, Naomi, you've been robbed."

Doug saw no point in running. Both women had identified him. It was too late. Besides, his head was throbbing and he was literally seeing stars.

The police arrived surprisingly quickly and, at the same time, Naomi's security guard appeared, weaving his way down the path to the front door.

"You're drunk!" Naomi shouted. "We could have been killed while you were out drinking!"

Visibly frightened and upset, the guard begged Naomi not to sack him. Doug was put in handcuffs and led to a police car outside. Ruth followed, stopping at the car, waiting for a chance to look Doug straight in the eye.

"Does the name Rachel Ross mean anything to you?" she cried at him as he refused to look, staring straight ahead of him.

Doug froze. "Ross!" Of course! Why did he not make the connection earlier?

***

Once out of sight of the bungalow, the police car pulled over to the side of the road. The driver turned to look straight at Doug in the back seat.

"Okay, how much do you want this time?" Doug asked.

Five minutes later, he stood alone at the side of Morogoro Road, completely penniless now and contemplating the long walk home. Worse than that, how was he going to get Christopher off his back? He began to walk.

Chapter 19

"Dear Isla,

At last I have the time to write to you! I wonder how things are there? Do you see much of my parents? When I speak to them they say everything is okay but I am worried about Dad especially. How's that new job of yours going? And how is the gorgeous boyfriend?

There's so much to tell you. I like it here. There is a lot of poverty, too much to tackle but once you've seen it you can't ignore it and you feel compelled to do something however small. The good thing is that generally everyone looks out for each other. The other day I got on a 'dala dala' – it's like a minibus with music blaring out of loud speakers at the back, a cheapish form of travel for locals that gets very overcrowded with people even hanging on to the roof racks on the outside. Anyway, a woman wanted to get on after me and she had two bags and a baby on her back, so she untied the sling that was holding her baby and without saying anything plonked her on my knee whilst she proceeded to find room to put the bags down. Totally sensible but can you ever imagine that happening on a bus in Dumfries? The other thing that happened on the same journey was really funny – there was an old man sitting right in front of me who kept turning around to stare at me – not many white people travel by dala dala – I just smiled at him and he turned back. Then, eventually he turned around again and put his hand over the back of his seat and sort of wiped my arm with his hand, causing everyone to laugh. I don't know, maybe he thought I had been painted and was black underneath!

I've met so many people in the short time I've been out here. Everyone seems really nice – I know, weak word – but when you're white, people are just nice to you, smiling and saying 'yes' to everything you say. It's hard to work out what people really think a lot of the time. It's not like that with my boss, Naomi. She's very straightforward. I really like her and I think she likes me. I've learned a lot from her and she's always looking out for me, warning me what to do and what not to do. The other day I was walking in the city centre and when I got back to the office I noticed my watch was missing – well, the face at least – the strap was still on my arm, stuck to it with sweat. It had been cleanly cut and the face stolen without me feeling a thing! Naomi told me not to wear jewellery, especially gold, when walking around. Apparently it's not unheard of for thieves to grab necklaces, bracelets and earrings from people stopped at traffic lights if their vehicle windows are open. 'Better not to advertise what you have,' Naomi said.

The poverty here is on another scale but people keep going, keep smiling and laughing. I asked Naomi whether there's much depression. She laughed and said, 'People here are too busy surviving to be depressed'."

Ruth paused, put down her pen and re-read what she had written. It was not at all what she wanted to say. She pushed the paper to one side, tore off a new sheet from her pad and started again:

"Dear Isla,

100

I don't know how to tell you what I am about to tell you so I am just going to plunge straight in…"

Ruth wrote down everything: how Doug was arrested; how she met Andi, and realising she was pregnant. The mere act of getting everything out of her head and onto paper felt cathartic. "I honestly can't believe I got myself into this situation," she wrote. "I've been here such a short time and you'd think I would have learned from what happened at home. I'm still trying to figure out how I could have been so careless but there's something about being here that just made me throw all caution to the wind – well, that and a shed load of alcohol. Thank God only Naomi knows. I don't know what the others would think if they knew. And I have no idea how I am going to tell Mum and Dad. "

Ruth went on. "Naomi was trying to insist I fly home but there is no way I am leaving her after what's happened. She's broken. She doesn't really want me to leave, I can tell. I did consider it briefly but what have I got to come back to? My reputation is shattered at the hospital and no doubt the powers that be would have made sure I don't get a job anywhere else in Dumfries so I'd have to move and start again somewhere else. Why not make that here? I need to stop running when things go wrong. I really think I can give this a go and I want to. This child is half Tanzanian. I need to give my life here a chance so that when he or she does arrive they can too. I don't know how we're going to manage but Naomi wants us to go to Dar es Salaam to find this rich relative of hers who she thinks will help her. It sounds a bit of a long shot to me but cultural traditions are very strongly abided to and this is one of them apparently so let's hope she's right.

We are going to Dar tomorrow by train. VSO have been really good. They sent someone up here from Dar to run the office and told Naomi to take as much time as she needs. They were fine about me too because they can see she shouldn't be alone. I'm feeling guilty about those kids though, I told them I'd go back and visit soon. Hopefully we won't be gone too long. We don't even have anywhere to stay yet. Luckily Naomi knows the place a bit."

Ruth finished off her letter and placed it to one side, ready to take or send into town later. She went out onto the veranda where she stood contemplating her surroundings. She was starting to understand that life in Tanzania had, very much, to be lived by faith. Absolutely nothing could be taken for granted and there was something in that fact which bound people together in a way that she had never experienced before.

"Some juice, madam?" Sylivia had arrived and was holding out a glass of papaya juice that Ruth took gratefully.

"Asante sana," she thanked Sylivia who did a sort of curtsey that made Ruth feel awkward. She thought she would never get used to that.

***

In the days following Doug's arrest, Naomi retreated into herself. She appeared to lose all energy, refused to get dressed and chose to spend a good deal of her time alone in her room in prayer.

Ruth remained patient. Filled with compassion for Naomi, she continued trying to be as normal as possible. With Sylivia's help, she bought food at the market and made sure a daily meal was provided, insisting that Sylivia taught her how to make ugali, rice and beans, something Sylivia found hilarious. She received visitors and made herself available should Naomi wish to talk, which was rare.

Thankfully, once Naomi decided to make the trip to Dar es Salaam, she began to surface a bit more often. She was grateful to Ruth and wanted to show her. Every now and again when she thought of the child Ruth was carrying – her grandchild – she even managed a smile.

There was hope.

Chapter 20

The evening before Ruth and Naomi left for Dar es Salaam, Naomi asked Gilbert to drive them down to the shores of Lake Victoria.

Aside from the occasional, slight undulation on her inky surface, the lake appeared unnervingly still. Only the intermittent threads of pale moonlight, escaping from behind the cloud cover, danced shakily on top of her sleek form.

The two women stood staring out at the great expanse, trying to conceive how this, now, gentle giant could have committed such a violent act, swallowing up hundreds of souls, in the cruel way she had.

It was some time before either of them spoke. Naomi was first to break the silence. She spoke in Kihaya. The words themselves meant nothing to Ruth but the sense was clear. This was an emotional goodbye to the three people closest to her in the world. Ruth stood as still as she could, her head bent respectfully. She pictured Andi's smiling face as he winked at her and her chest hurt. At that moment she had no idea what her future would look like but she knew that, because of the life growing inside her, Andi would always be a part of it.

Eventually, Naomi turned to Ruth.

"Twende tu," she said, turning to walk back up the shore to where Gilbert was waiting for them.

Ruth followed.

***

The train journey to Dar es Salaam took two days and was not uneventful. Overwhelmed by the heat and smell of fried food, Ruth spent the entire journey feeling extremely nauseous. Naomi remained quiet for the most part. In contrast to Ruth, she spent much of the time sleeping. She disembarked once in Dodoma to buy them food from one of the many tin shed stalls adjacent to their platform. Ruth could not face eating anything, so Naomi slowly made her way through two portions of fried chicken with piri piri sauce, washed down with a bottle of tangawizi soda. Ruth followed suit with the soda, relishing the combination of its sharp ginger flavour and fizziness that made her want to burp out loud.

Having been warned to shut their carriage windows at night as a deterrent to thieves, Naomi did so, leaving Ruth feeling that she was about to expire. She had never known heat like it. The only thing she could do was wave her hand in front of her face, an act that had little effect other than to raise a smile on the faces of amused fellow passengers.

On the odd occasion that Naomi was awake, Ruth noticed how easily she fell into conversation with the people around. Several of them were clearly seasoned travellers. They had brought large amounts of cooked food with them and proceeded to lay it all out on cloths for everyone to share. At night, whatever was left was tightly wrapped up again to avoid attracting rodents they knew would come scavenging for scraps. Two women in Naomi and Ruth's carriage sat on a foldaway 'bed', one between the other's legs, the other braiding her hair, both chattering loudly as the train rattled along.

If the heat and the motion sickness proved difficult to bear, compensation came in the form of what Ruth could see out of the window. The train virtually ambled along, passing village after village of mud-walled, thatched-roof huts flanked by tall, lush banana groves. Ruth recalled Naomi's stories of her school days in Bukoba and how her mother used to wrap the children's food in a banana leaf to keep it fresh and clean.

In between villages, the train picked up pace a little as it eased its way over vast, uninterrupted areas of grassland, an occasional, unmistakably long neck of a giraffe in the distance, standing and staring warily at the monster chugging by.

Being the outsider and unable to speak Swahili, Ruth had to sit and observe. She was getting used to the sound of the language and recognised some of the more commonly used words and phrases and even attempted to employ one or two herself when the opportunity came. The response to her efforts, she found, was an initial spurt of great delight, usually followed by a long involved sentence, which she didn't understand a word of, resulting in a trailing-off of that initial delight and a conversation lost forever. Learning Swahili was going to be crucial to Ruth.

On their arrival at the Central Railway Station in Dar es Salaam, Naomi took charge. Armed with the name of a local hostel – a tip from a fellow traveller – and her rough knowledge of the city, she weaved her way wearily through the dusty streets with Ruth at her heels. Carrying their heavy bags, they walked along India Street and into Mosque Street, passed a Taj Mahal Shop and finally into Jamhuri Street where they found the Sleep Inn Hotel.

All Ruth wanted was some cold water to drink and a bed to lie on. She got the bed but drinking water was more of a problem. According to the inn owner, one of the main pipes connecting their part of the city to a water supply had cracked in the heat and now the rains were delaying its repair. Naomi negotiated with him for his young son to run and buy them some bottled water.

The women shared a room on the second floor. It was sparsely furnished with two single beds, each with a thin mattress and sheet, a vast helicopter fan in the centre of the ceiling and one bedside cabinet whose cupboard door was jammed shut. The small window was broken and the slatted blind stuck fast halfway down. A miniscule WC cubicle led off from the room. It had a shower that you could "swing a dog in," as Naomi pointed out, a small sink and a toilet. There was no soap and no towel. The toilet paper was like Ruth remembered from her very early primary school days – brittle and shiny on one side and absolutely no use at all. None of this mattered; all she wanted to do was stretch flat out under that fan.

From her horizontal position, Ruth watched Naomi closely. Visibly thinner and lacking the gusto she had radiated when they first met, Naomi appeared, to Ruth, to be shrinking. Ruth watched her pull a scarf over her head and kneel to pray in familiar ritual. Ruth waited. Naomi mumbled, quietly at first, then her voice became louder, finally reaching a loud and passionate cry for help. Ruth thought it was odd that an intelligent person like Naomi could put so much faith and trust into something she could neither see nor touch.

"Are you not angry with God?" Ruth asked when Naomi had finished praying.

"Angry?" Naomi looked surprised. "No," she said.

"But how do you make sense of it all?" Ruth persisted.

"It's not my job to make sense of it. Many people want to blame God when they are suffering. But God does not send misery. Bad things happen. It's the world we live in. God helps us to deal with them. Without him we are nothing."

There was finality in Naomi's words that persuaded Ruth it was not the time to pursue her questions.

Before sleeping, Naomi rooted around in her kiondo. The bag held so much it took a while to locate the folded piece of paper she had slipped into it prior to leaving Mwanza. Unfolding it, she read, for the umpteenth time, the scribbled words that were written on it:

'Bwana Kai Bouchard
Kilimanjaro Hotel'

"He is your cousin", her mother had told her on that last visit to Bukoba, before she passed away. "He has come back home. He's a very wealthy man. He will surely help you if you ever need it."

Naomi took the paper to please her mother though she had doubted she would ever use it. People came to her and Salva for help; she was used to that. How could she possibly have foreseen the direction her life would take?

Naomi knew she had to do something. The money she and Ruth had would not last long, and she was beginning to feel really weak. Her head ached most of the time, she was losing weight and her appetite was very low. She had a feeling that whatever was wrong was not grief alone. If they needed to buy medicines as well, they were going to be in deep trouble very soon. Glancing over to the other bed, Naomi observed her sleeping companion. Ruth was now their only hope.

Chapter 21

Kai Bouchard was a businessman but he was also a philanthropist. He knew what it meant to straddle two cultures. A product of his Tanzanian mother and Canadian father, he spent his early childhood running around barefoot with the other kids in Mbezi beach before his diplomat father had insisted he continue his education in Montreal where he would become bilingual, gain a string of letters after his name and receive numerous awards for his academic and sporting achievements.

In fact, there was only one thing in Kai's life that he had not been successful at and that was his marriage. His former wife referred to herself as a widow. She filed for divorce on the grounds that he was married to his high-flying executive banking job and claimed half of everything they owned together, including the beautiful lakeside mansion Kai had designed and had built for them, thinking it would be the perfect family home.

Kai was willing to concede that he had been a workaholic and with the benefit of hindsight recognised that a person could become very lonely waiting around every day, so he did not blame his ex-wife for feeling the way she did. However, it did not sit comfortably with him that she had managed to get her hands on as much as she had. After all, it was his salary that had enabled them to live the luxurious lifestyle they had. She had chosen not to work, preferring to spend her days lunching and shopping with the other wives, something that surprised him and made him wonder if he had made a wise choice in the first place. Kai had given in to her demands. Let her have what she wanted, he reasoned. He knew it would not bring her happiness in the long run, and they had loved each other once. He, on the other hand, would prefer to walk away while he still could.

It was at that point in his life he had decided to move back to live in Dar es Salaam. It was an easy transition. He spoke Swahili and had many friends in Dar as he visited every year with his mother first before she passed away and a few times after that but always alone, his dad saying it was too painful and choosing to stay in Canada.

Hailing from Montreal, Kai was a fluent French speaker and had learned Italian and German too. With his Swahili to boot and tourism being the fastest growing sector in Tanzania, it seemed the most obvious career choice. He was still a rich man in spite of the losses and he purchased a hotel. Not just any hotel; he bought the Kilimanjaro hotel and he was making a great success out of it.

The Kili, as it was known locally, was clearly a profit-making machine, but Kai used it also as a venue for all kinds of altruistic purposes. He hosted concerts with the likes of Youssou N'dour, Ladysmith Black Mambazo and Miriam Makeba, selling tickets at affordable prices and asking his business friends to purchase extra to give away to community-based organisations so young people, who would normally never be able to attend, could hear these famous African musicians. He provided a room, stage and equipment free of charge for retailers who wanted to hold fashion shows on condition that they donate twenty per cent of all sales to local charities chosen by a public voting system run across the city.

Kai did not just do things randomly. He ran his charitable activities like another business with checks and balances in place, recording everything meticulously so that he could review the impact of his actions and formulate new ideas accordingly. He did not want to be associated with the corruption he knew existed in some sectors, so he insisted on being transparent and accountable. Because of this, Kai was well liked and generally people did not try to cheat him as they felt that, sooner or later, they, or someone in their family, would benefit from one of Bwana Kai Bouchard's initiatives.

Kai's portrait was a regular in the Dar es Salaam newspapers. Recognising that he had to maintain a high profile if he wanted to achieve social change of any sort, he did not actively court it and he never, ever spoke about his personal life to anyone. He had accepted his part in the failure of his marriage and he carried that guilt. He knew it had hurt his mother deeply and he had no intention of hurting anyone else. With this attitude Kai had been getting along just fine for the past few years.

It was now time for the annual book fayre in Dar es Salaam and Kai looked with pride upon the immaculately groomed grounds and freshly whitewashed pillars and walls of his hotel. 'His hotel', the words still sounded as pleasing to him now as on the day he first took it over. In less than forty-eight hours the place would be teeming with delegates from all over Southern Africa, all converging on this beautiful venue to network, promote and, most importantly, to sell their books.

"Bwana Bouchardee!"

Kai recognised the clip-clapping of Rose's heels on the marbled floor. He turned to greet his events manager who approached him armed with an over-filled lever arch file clearly labelled 'Book Fayre'.

"Habari za asubuhi, Bwana Bouchardee?"

"Salaama tu. Habari yako?" Kai assured Rose he was fine and enquired how she was.

Switching into English, as was her way, Rose continued. "Please, Bwana, I just need to ask you to sign off on these payment requests."

Kai took the bits of paper Rose handed him. "Okay, so these are the goody bags for the children's day," he confirmed.

"That's right, Bwana. We are going to start packaging them up this afternoon."

"Have you had many responses to the ads for casual staff?" Kai enquired.

"Oh yes, Bwana. There have been many. We have hired some and are checking others through."

"Okay, leave it up for today and let me know what happens, please. Thank uou, Rose. Very efficient as always."

Rose looked pleased with herself as she bustled away, her folder nestled under her arm like a precious baby.

Chapter 22

Ruth and Naomi had been awake for some time. The early morning wailing call to prayer, booming across a rousing city, had woken them both. Disoriented at first, Ruth lay listening to the still strange sounds whilst her waking mind grappled to make sense of her surroundings.

"I need you to do something," Naomi announced.

"Of course. Name it," Ruth responded without hesitation.

"There was an advert I saw on the way to this place yesterday. It was asking for people to work at the book fayre in the Kilimanjaro hotel."

Ruth was confused. Why did she need to work? Weren't they here to find someone?

"We could be here for a while. We will need money for food and to pay this man here. If you can get a temporary job, I can be looking for my relative whilst you are working."

Ruth didn't argue. It would not hurt her to keep occupied, and Naomi was right about the money. She dressed and went out, following the directions Naomi had given her.

The city heat was overwhelming and Ruth soon felt her energy sapping. By the time she arrived outside the Kilimanjaro she was parched. She bought a soda from a stall on the pavement outside the hotel and stood drinking it under a tree before returning the glass bottle and lid to the stall holder.

"Karibu tena," the woman said, inviting Ruth to return, with a grin that revealed more gaps than teeth.

Once inside the hotel, Ruth began to feel human again. She made enquiries at the reception desk where she was asked to wait and someone would come.

After ten minutes or so, a smartly dressed woman appeared, her hair neatly scraped back into an efficient bun, carrying a clipboard in one hand and a pen in the other, her stiletto heels click-clacking along as she approached Ruth.

"Good morning, madam. I am Rose. I am events manager here at the Kilimanjaro hotel."

The woman spoke slowly and deliberately with a heavy accent.

Ruth returned the greeting and at Rose's request, followed her down a corridor off the main foyer and into a small, bright office where she was offered a seat and asked if she would like to take some "chai", which she gratefully accepted, secretly hoping it would be made with condensed milk.

Rose Msoka was delighted that she had her first Mzungu applicant. Just wait until Bwana Bouchardee found out! There was no question in Rose's mind that Ruth would be hired, but she was a stickler for following procedures and besides, she wanted this Mzungu lady to know that Tanzanians could be professional and do things in an orderly manner. The country might often be jokingly referred to as "Bongo Land" by locals but that didn't mean that things could not be smooth and efficient, especially if Rose Msoka had anything to do with it.

Two hours and several cups of chai later – no one was going to rush Rose Msoka – they emerged from Rose's office, Ruth clutching her patriotic blue, green, yellow and white striped lanyard with identification badge and official programme for the week to come.

"I will show you around our hotel and introduce you to the team you will be working with," Rose announced importantly. "Let's go outside first, by the pool."

Walking alongside the length of the pool, Ruth imagined herself stripping off there and then and diving into the stunningly blue water that dazzled her as the sun's rays met its translucent surface. They rounded a corner and Rose's attention was suddenly diverted.

"Oh, Bwana Bouchardee, we have a new recruit!" she called out to a man who had his back to them walking away. The man stopped, turned around and smiled.

"Hi there. Welcome to the Kilimanjaro," he said, offering his hand to Ruth. He spoke with an American or Canadian accent. Ruth was never quite sure of the difference.

"Hello, I'm Ruth."

"Nice to meet you Ruth. So glad you can join us." Ruth noticed the man had kind eyes that took time to meet hers in a way that made her feel she was really being taken notice of. Though wearing a suit, he was relaxed and stood with one hand in his pocket and the other distractedly stroking his goatee. He was probably mid-forties and

116

handsome. He wore a crisp white shirt under his jacket, no tie just a stylish grandad collar. His coffee-toned skin colour marked him out as different amongst the black and white faces generally seen around. Ruth caught sight of his name badge – Kai Bouchard – not a Tanzanian name, she was sure of that. French perhaps.

"Well, Bwana Bouchardee, we cannot stand and chat all day. I need to show Miss Ruth around so she can get started. We must get on now."

Kai stepped aside with a knowing smile as Rose indicated for Ruth to follow her. It was important to Rose that the "big boss" could see she meant business. "That is Bwana Bouchardee," she announced. "He is the owner of this magnificent hotel." Rose's voice became almost majestic as she spoke these last words, looking around and nodding with approval and pride at her surroundings as though they belonged to her too.

***

Naomi did not feel good at all. Her head hurt every time she moved and her throat had begun to sting. She was weak and, despite good intentions, had not even made it out of the room she and Ruth were sharing. Towards lunchtime she started to shiver with cold so she wrapped herself in a kanga and lay down on the bed. This is how Ruth found her on returning from her first day at the Kilimanjaro hotel.

"Naomi! What's wrong?" Ruth was concerned and wanted to send the inn owner's son for medicine, but Naomi insisted they wait until the following day.

"It is probably just a mild dose of malaria," Naomi said. "It will pass. I just need to rest."

Worried, Ruth sat next to Naomi, who shortly fell asleep.

Ruth did not like it; after all Rwehema died from malaria. However, she respected Naomi and decided to follow her wishes, for the time being, at least. It was clear to Ruth that if there was no improvement, she would need to find a doctor.

For the next few days, Ruth had to leave early in the morning and return late in the evening. She gave instructions to the inn owner and his wife to keep close watch over Naomi, which they were happy to do, refusing to take the money she offered them. Ruth bought painkillers from the pharmacy at the Kilimanjaro hotel to relieve Naomi's head and body aches.

By Saturday, Naomi was barely speaking. Confined to her bed, she was eating and drinking very little. Her body was becoming thinner and frailer, and Ruth knew she had to do something. The inn owner instructed his son to go to the hospital where a friend worked and ask him to bring a doctor. They waited all day. Ruth did not go to the hotel; she could not desert her companion. Instead, she sat by her side talking softly to her and patting her forehead with a cool rag. Naomi was burning up. The doctor, who was unable to leave the hospital until after his shift, arrived in the evening. "We need to get her into hospital," he said after a quick examination. "She is very sick."

It was after midnight when Ruth finally returned from the hospital. She had wanted to stay but there was nowhere for her to sit close to Naomi. People were very kind but she had eyes; she could see how under-resourced the hospital was.

Alone in the room, with Naomi's belongings, Ruth began to feel isolated and terribly alone.

'What now?' she thought.

Chapter 23

The book fayre was a great success and after it was over, Rose offered Ruth a job as a chamber maid, which Ruth accepted without hesitation. Her income was the only way she would be able to survive now and the only way Naomi could continue to receive help. The job was not as bad as Ruth feared. She got on well with the other 'maids' and the work was okay as long as she focused on one room at a time and did not get bogged down with the mindless tasks that had to be repeated hundreds of times over. Besides, she had chance to see how the other half was living – some of the views from the top floor right across the city were incredible – giving her a totally new perspective on this huge conglomeration they had named 'Haven of Peace.'

Every day after work, Ruth walked back to her room at the inn via the hospital. She sat for a long time on Naomi's bed, sometimes reading from the small bible she had picked up out of her friend's kiondo. "Come on, God," she whispered. "Now is the time to show Naomi what you can do."

Wearily, Ruth arrived back at the inn where she counted her day's earnings and separated out what she needed for food and what was for Naomi's care. She had overheard another maid talking about the new Aga Khan hospital. It was costly, by all accounts, but modern and well equipped. Ruth was determined to get Naomi in there as soon as she had saved enough money.

***

One morning, Rose appeared in the room Ruth was in the process of cleaning at the hotel.

"Miss Ruth, can you come with me, please?"

"What is it?" Ruth asked.

"Just come with me and I will explain. Thank you."

The two women walked the length of the corridor in silence and entered Rose's office. Rose closed the door behind them, turned to face Ruth and said, "Now, Miss Ruth, we have had a complaint made against you."

"What sort of complaint?" Ruth was surprised.

"One of our guests claims an expensive bracelet went missing from her room during your shift."

"Oh, well, that's okay because I know I haven't taken it so there must be another simple explanation. Shall we help her look for it?" Ruth replied, unconcerned.

"I am afraid it is not as simple as you think. This guest is adamant that we open your locker in her presence."

"That's fine. You will find nothing but if that's what she wants," Ruth said, a little taken aback.

Rose and Ruth made their way to the locker room. As they arrived, a slim, blonde woman was waiting for them by the door. Ruth could not believe her eyes. What on earth was Freja doing here?

121

Freja Johansson was enjoying herself. The sheer shock on Ruth's face was enough to make the miserable flight to Dar es Salaam worth every minute.

"Hello, Freja," Ruth said cautiously.

"Do you two ladies know each other?" Rose interrupted.

"I'm sorry," Freja said, "I have never seen this woman before in my life."

"What!" Ruth was incredulous. Even Freja could not stoop so low, surely.

Freja smiled condescendingly, "You must be mixing me up with someone else. There are quite a few of us Danes in the country."

"This is crazy. I know this woman!" Ruth insisted.

Rose intervened. "Madame Erikson," she said, looking at Freja, "please tell our chamber maid what you told me."

Freja played the role perfectly, and there was nothing at all Ruth could do. The bracelet in question was found in Ruth's locker, and she was promptly and unceremoniously dismissed on the spot.

***

Think, think, think. Ruth walked aimlessly away from the hotel, trying to make sense of what just happened. What was she going to do now? How could she continue to help Naomi without any money and what about the child inside her? She had to think of something. Who was this relative that Naomi came to Da es Salaam to look for? He might be the only one who could help her now. Freja could wait.

It was mid-afternoon when Ruth reached the hospital, her head full of the happenings at the hotel. Intent on seeing Naomi, Ruth wove her way through the familiar queues of people lining the paths leading up to the main entrance. She had become accustomed to seeing people sitting and lying inside and outside while they waited in the hope of medical attention for themselves or a loved one. Ruth reached Naomi's bed but someone else, not Naomi, lay helpless on it.

A nervous energy surging through her body, Ruth searched around for a familiar face. One of the nurses rushed past her and as she did so her eyes met Ruth's. On the point of enquiring after the whereabouts of her friend, Ruth stopped in her tracks, the question left hanging on her lips; that look in the nurse's eyes, as she shook her head, was enough; Ruth had no need to ask it.

"Oh no, no!" Ruth heard her own moans as the meaning of those head shakes became clear and her body crumpled to the floor. "Why, Naomi? Why now?"

Chapter 24

"What happened to the Scottish girl?" Kai enquired of Rose on Monday morning.

Uncomfortably, Rose explained to him what had transpired.

Kai listened carefully. He wished the matter had been referred to him but he was a practical man who believed in dealing with the here and now. "That is strange," he said. "Why would Ruth say she knew someone if she didn't? It doesn't make any sense. Do you have any contact details for her? I would like to follow this one up. There's something not quite fitting here."

Rose was uncharacteristically flustered. Had she got it wrong?

***

In the hospital, Ruth was led to the place where Naomi's body lay amidst others recently deceased. She looked peaceful, her ashen face framed by the pretty kanga she had been wearing. What a contrast to the day Ruth first arrived in Mwanza.

Someone was speaking to Ruth. She caught the words, "…We can only release the body to a family member." All she could do was stare at the mouth of the doctor who spoke to her. She heard what he was saying but was unable to process the words.

Ruth did not remember leaving the hospital or how she arrived back at the inn where she found herself some time later, a flask of tea beside her bed. She sat for a very long time staring at Naomi's bed and her kiondo – all that remained in place of her friend. Eventually she lay down on her side, instinctively curling up into a protective ball. Then the tears came.

***

Kai had no luck with finding out more about Ruth so he decided to focus his attention on the Erikson woman. Nothing matching her profile was coming up when he searched the internet. Rose handed him a picture that was taken in the dining room during Miss Erikson's stay. It was promotional material for their brochure taken with full permission of those appearing in it. Kai had many contacts amongst the expatriate community in Dar es Salaam. He would show the photograph around and see if anyone recognised this 'Miss Erikson'.

***

Feeling completely desolate, Ruth did not emerge from her room for two days. The inn owner's wife brought her tea and samosas. Ruth had no desire for food but she had to consider the life inside her. Her head was spinning. Here she was in a strange city in a foreign country, totally alone.

Apart from Naomi's relative, who she had no way of contacting, there was only one person she could think of whose number she had somewhere and who was certainly indebted to her. It was worth a try.

Doug recognised the number flashing up on his cell phone.

"Hello," he said hesitantly.

"Hello, Doug. You're not in prison then?"

There was a long pause.

"Look, Doug, I need help and you owe me, you owe me big time."

Doug listened warily. He was very fond of Naomi and the news of her passing shocked him. Of course he would do everything he could to help locate a family member in Bukoba and bring them to Dar so that her body could be released for a traditional burial. He had no idea how he would achieve it. All of that would take money and he had very little. But he sure as hell was going to bust a gut to try.

"Oh, and Doug, Naomi forgave you for what you did. If it was me it would have been a different matter."

Silence on the line.

"You know, Ruth, I didn't know she was dead until after I left." Doug was no longer referring to Naomi. He continued. "She looked me straight in the eyes, just before impact. I panicked, Ruth. I was eighteen years old. I ran and I just kept running. I ran so far that I couldn't go back."

There was another long pause.

"There isn't a day that goes past when I don't think of her. You have to know how sorry I am."

126

Ruth did not want to think about Rachel.

"Just help me get Naomi back where she belongs," she said. "If you mean what you say, when this is all over you can face my parents and tell them what you just told me."

The more she thought about what had happened at the hotel, the more angry she felt. She kept remembering the eyes of Bwana Bouchard. He looked like a man who would want to know. Unwilling to simply wait for Doug to act, she began to formulate a plan.

Chapter 25

Ruth walked into the Kilimanjaro hotel, her head held high. One of the receptionists led her to Kai's office and on the way they passed Rose Msoka's room. The door was open and Rose looked up from her desk. Ruth continued, looking straight ahead.

"Hi, Ruth, so glad you came back." Kai was welcoming, putting Ruth at ease.

"Good morning, Mr Bouchard. Thank you for agreeing to see me."

"Actually, I have been looking for you. I wanted to hear your side of the story."

It was so easy talking to Kai Bouchard. Ruth could see immediately why he was so popular. He listened attentively, not interrupting, and you could almost see his mind working as he concentrated on what he was being told.

"If, as you say, this Freja's father is DANIDA rep here in Dar, it shouldn't be difficult to check," he commented when Ruth had finished.

"She will only deny what happened, just like she denied knowing me."

Reaching into his desk drawer, Kai pulled out the photograph Rose had handed him and showed it to Ruth.

"She can't deny this, can she?"

Ruth agreed they had solid proof Freja was at the hotel and the date she was photographed but that didn't help with the bracelet incident and Freja could wriggle out of anything. The only witness was Rose and she was Tanzanian. Freja had a low opinion of Africans generally, believing them to be cheats and liars. She would use that somehow to twist things. It was time for Ruth to introduce her proposal.

"How about you find some reason to call her back in – just getting a signature from her that was overlooked or something – I can wait outside and intercept her as she's leaving. I'll ask her straight why she did what she did and hopefully catch her out that way because she won't think anyone can hear her. If I record our conversation, then we'll have her."

Kai was impressed. He would not normally approve of such methods but this was not a normal situation.

"Just tell me, why would she do this to you?" he asked.

Having nothing to lose, Ruth told Kai about Andi.

A plan was finalised and they shook on it. Ruth got up to leave but had to sit down again.

"Are you okay? You look as white as a sheet," Kai said, concerned.

Without thinking, Ruth rubbed her belly.

"Are you unwell?" Kai asked.

Ruth was suddenly overcome with fatigue.

"Can I just sit here a little longer?"

"Sure you can. I'll get you another drink." Kai disappeared and quickly returned carrying a mug of hot tea. It was sweet, made with condensed milk, just as in Mwanza. That made Ruth cry.

A little shocked, Kai looked at Ruth, trying to work out what was going on. Giving her time to compose herself, he sat quietly at first, then he spoke.

"Do you want to talk about it?" he asked with genuine interest.

Ruth found the words to tell Kai about Naomi and her plans to return her body to Bukoba. She also told him about the baby and the ferry disaster. As she talked, she noticed Kai's expression change from one of concern to one of recognition, particularly when she mentioned Salva, Julius and Andi.

"You said Naomi hails from Bukoba?" Kai confirmed.

"Yes. She must still have family there. I have never been but I owe it to them to get her back."

"What is Naomi's family name?"

"Rweyamamu I think... yes. Her married name was Rwechungura."

Kai sat up straight.

"I'm not certain. I need to check this out but there is a very strong chance you are talking about my relatives," he said.

Chapter 26

Freja was feeling pleased with herself. She had just had her hair done by Birgitte – a top stylist brought out especially from Denmark to style the DANIDA staff hair – she had a new dress and her tan was nicely topped up after a few sessions by the hotel pool. She breezed out of the hotel lobby, stylishly pulling her sunglasses down from the crown of her head and paused to consider where she should go next.

"Hello, Freja."

Freja turned sharply and saw Ruth standing in front of her. She smirked. How tedious, she thought.

"Hello, Ruth. How are things? Not too unemployed I hope."

This could not have gone better, thought Ruth. She is playing right into my hands.

"What was all that about, Freja?"

"Well, since you ask," Freja quickly glanced around her before continuing. "You swan over here like little Miss Perfect, pretending you care so much about the Africans, making everybody love you. But you don't stop there. Oh no, you set your sights on *my* Andi. Well, that was too much. Nobody takes my man and gets away with it." Not being able to resist an extra dig, Freja added, "You know the best part? It was so easy getting one of those silly chamber maids to leave the bracelet in your locker."

"He's dead, Freja. Is that not enough for you?"

Freja snorted. "At least I know you can't have him either."

"Oh well," Ruth sighed. "It doesn't matter now. What's done is done." She turned to leave then turned back and, placing a hand on her belly, she said, "A part of him will always be with me."

Ruth walked away, leaving Freja standing open-mouthed behind her.

Heading straight for Kai's office, Ruth handed him the evidence. "Since you now know that I didn't steal, can I have my job back?" she asked.

Admiring her tenacity, Kai agreed to let Ruth continue working in the hotel.

"Given your background, how about community liaison assistant? You would be working under Rose, of course."

"Sounds great," Ruth said. "But first I need to request some leave to take a very important trip."

Kai smiled. In the circumstances, with the information he had gathered about his extended family, he could hardly refuse.

***

'Dear Isla,

I am so sorry it's been a while since I wrote. I hope you'll forgive me. So much has happened again…'

As she wrote, Ruth found solace in the words. She relived the events of the past weeks with sadness. Naomi had been so special to Ruth. Their friendship had blossomed quickly. They trusted each other, were honest with each other and, most of all, respected each other. That was hard to come by, especially when you came from two completely different cultures. Now that Naomi was gone, Ruth owed it to her to carry on her legacy: to keep striving to give a voice to those who had no voice.

Ruth gently rubbed her now well-rounded belly. This child would, tragically, never meet its grandmother, but Ruth would make damn sure he or she knew her.

'The traditional burial was so moving, Isla! And the wailing! Such a powerful sound. So many people attended. I would not have been able to go without Kai's help; he bought the plane tickets. Luckily I was still okay to fly. Everyone was incredibly sad about Naomi, especially after what happened with Salva and the boys too but they were overjoyed to see Kai and welcomed him like the prodigal son! With his help, we were able to organise enough food and drink for everyone. I think the whole village came out and maybe even some from neighbouring villages. I felt so insignificant.

Doug was there but I kept my distance. He had played his part in letting the relatives know what had happened. It wasn't the place for us to talk. That will have to come later.

Kai found the whole thing extremely moving. I think it brought back memories of his late mum. He's made so many new connections there now that he's never going to lose. Do you know, there were loads of children outside begging for our food? When we spoke to them we found out they were orphans; their parents died of AIDS so Kai organised some local women – volunteers – to cook a daily meal for them as a start. One of his cousins is going to keep an eye on them for him. I've got a feeling he will be going back there often. He seems to have big plans.

I think about Naomi every day. I had to go through her things. There wasn't much left. I think relatives took the house in Mwanza. I was told I could have her kiondo bag and its contents. Inside I found Kai's name and the hotel name scribbled on a folded piece of paper. Naomi knew what she was doing when she sent me to the Kilimanjaro yet she never said a word.

I miss you all. I did speak to Mum and Dad and I plucked up the courage to tell them about the baby. I still haven't told them about Doug. It seemed cruel when they were so thrilled about my first piece of news. I didn't expect that. It made me feel better. Of course, they want me to come home for the birth but I want to do it here with other women, not isolate myself to somewhere because they feel it's "safer" and "cleaner".

Not long to go now. Any chance of you making the trip out here?'

Chapter 27

On 21 July 2000, Sekelaga Naomi Ross was born in Dar es Salaam.

Ruth wept. Looking into the child's face, she felt hope for their future yet, at the same time, deep sadness, when she pictured the absent ones; those the child would never meet though they were so much part of the story leading up to her birth.

It had been a long labour, culminating in some complications for Ruth but the pain of childbirth was fleeting and she was left feeling exhausted, yet elated. Ruth studied her daughter's face as the little one slept innocently in her arms. She looked over to the single chair at the side of her bed where the clothes she arrived in were draped. Neatly placed, side by side, on top of the chair seat were the sandals she had bought in Kivukoni. Open-toed with two wide leather straps crisscrossed over the top, they were comfortable and moulded to the contours of her feet, whilst allowing them to breathe. A far cry from the highly unsuitable red, high-heeled strappy things she wore on her arrival into Africa, the sandals symbolised a transformation that Ruth could only think of as assimilation into her surroundings and it pleased her to look at them so.

The town flat Ruth was renting was no palace but it, at least, had electricity and running water – on and off. Rose, who showed herself to be a loyal friend, cleaned it thoroughly before Ruth moved in. "If you want to bring a mtoto here, the place must be spotless," she said. It was Rose, too, who organised a small baby shower in the gardens of the Kilimanjaro hotel, where Ruth found herself the recipient of several useful baby items as well as one or two very cute outfits ahead of the birth.

"Hodi!" Kai's voice interrupted Ruth's daydream.

"Karibu," she answered, welcoming him now in Swahili.

"You look well," he said as he held out his arms to take, the still sleeping, Sekelaga. "And you, young lady, I'm your uncle Kai. Welcome to the world."

Ruth and Kai chatted companionably. Ruth knew he was a big factor in her decision to stay around. His presence, somehow, took the fear of what was still a huge unknown to her: a world without Naomi. She was still determined to make her own way but knowing there was someone, who was related to her deceased friend, made a difference in a good way.

Later, when Kai left the hospital, he headed home to his bungalow in Mbezi beach. Driving along the coast road, he smelt the saltiness of the Indian Ocean as its waves lapped the white sands. Huge palms lined the shore, boasting ripe coconuts that they would not let go lightly. A young boy shinnied up a nobbled trunk, machete in one hand, poised to strike but before he dealt the blow, he called out to his companion on the beach below, telling him to catch or move out of the way. Kai smiled. He had been hit on the head by a coconut before; it was no small pain.

Kai was content with his life, yet Ruth's presence in Dar and his trip to Bukoba had reminded him there was something missing. It was tempting to want to step in and take care of Ruth and Seke but Kai knew Ruth was not looking for a saviour. No, he would have to content himself with being the good uncle. Ruth was just at the beginning of her journey. Her life had changed dramatically and she needed to figure out her place in the world. Kai knew that. He continued on his way, smiling to himself as he visualised the wooden dolls' house he had started building for the new arrival. It was coming on well.

***

Ruth reached for Naomi's kiondo once again. It was hers now and she took it everywhere. Feeling around inside the bag, she pulled out a piece of old, lined paper. She read the handwritten note to her daughter for the third time that day:

'Mjukuu wangu
Always remember you are precious in God's eyes.
Your Grandmother, Naomi.'
If only…

Ruth fought back the tears. This was not the time. Now she had to put all her energy into looking forward. Big challenges lay ahead, that was certainly true. But Ruth was now no longer alone in the world.

***

Somewhere, far from Dar es Salaam, across the great expanse of Lake Victoria into north western Tanzania, a young woman sat on the rust-coloured soil outside her father's hut, whilst he lay sick inside. Manona glanced over at her little girl, who was oblivious to life's cares, playing in the dirt. Kemi was two now. It was several months since they lost Andi, and the plans he and her mother had made together would never come to fruition. As long as her own father was sick, Manona had to stay put but as soon as she was able, she vowed she would be making the same trip across the water that had claimed Andi's life. It was her only chance of providing some kind of future for their daughter.